"You are carryin[g] [the] Ortega fortune. I want our child to be born legitimately. Can you really deny the baby his birthright?"

"It's not just a question of getting married," Rachel muttered. "I'd have to move to the other side of the world, to a strange country...."

"Argentina is not a strange country," Diego assured her, his mouth curving into a sudden smile that made her heart turn over. "It is a beautiful, vibrant country, and I promise you will fall in love with it, *querida*."

"When were you thinking of getting married?" she asked, her hand straying to her stomach.

Diego placed his hand next to hers. "I'll make the necessary arrangements immediately," he said. "We don't have much time."

CHANTELLE SHAW lives on the Kent coast, five minutes from the sea, and does much of her thinking about the characters in her books while walking on the beach. An avid reader from an early age, she found that school friends used to hide their books when she visited, but Chantelle would retreat into her own world and still writes stories in her head all the time.

Chantelle has been blissfully married to her own tall, dark and very patient hero for more than twenty years and has six children. She began to read Harlequin® Presents novels as a teenager, and throughout the years of being a stay-at-home mum to her brood, she found romance fiction helped her to stay sane! Her aim is to write books that provide an element of escapism, fun and of course romance for the countless women who juggle work and a home life and who need their precious moments of me time. She enjoys reading and writing about strong-willed, feisty women and even stronger-willed sexy heroes.

Chantelle is at her happiest when writing. She is particularly inspired while cooking dinner, which unfortunately results in a lot of culinary disasters! She also loves gardening, taking her very badly behaved terrier for walks and eating chocolate (followed by more walking—at least the dog is slim!).

ARGENTINIAN PLAYBOY, UNEXPECTED LOVE-CHILD

CHANTELLE SHAW

~ TAKEN: AT THE BOSS'S COMMAND ~

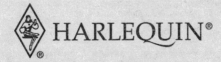

HARLEQUIN®

TORONTO • NEW YORK • LONDON
AMSTERDAM • PARIS • SYDNEY • HAMBURG
STOCKHOLM • ATHENS • TOKYO • MILAN • MADRID
PRAGUE • WARSAW • BUDAPEST • AUCKLAND

Recycling programs
for this product may
not exist in your area.

ISBN-13: 978-0-373-52734-2

ARGENTINIAN PLAYBOY, UNEXPECTED LOVE-CHILD

First North American Publication 2009.

Copyright © 2009 by Chantelle Shaw.

ARGENTINIAN PLAYBOY, UNEXPECTED LOVE-CHILD

CHAPTER ONE

DIEGO leaned against the paddock fence, his dark eyes narrowed against the glare of the early evening sun as he watched the horse and rider soar over the triple jump with impressive ease. The six foot wall was next. The horse was gathering pace and the rider stretched forwards along its neck in preparation for the jump.

The display of riding skill was fascinating to watch. Unwittingly, Diego held his breath, waiting for the horse's hooves to leave the ground. But at that moment a motorbike emerged from the woods, the high-pitched scream of its engine shattering the quiet air. The bike braked on the track which ran alongside the paddock with a squeal of tyres. The horse was clearly scared by the noise, and Diego knew instantly that it would refuse the jump. But there was nothing he could do, and he watched helplessly as the rider was thrown out of the saddle, sailed over the horse's head, and landed with a sickening thud on the sun-baked earth.

Rachel was winded by the force of the impact with the ground and she struggled to draw oxygen into her lungs. Her head was spinning and sensation was returning to her body, bringing with it various points of pain on her arms, shoulders, hips… She was going to have some spectacular bruises, she thought ruefully. It seemed easier to keep her eyes closed and sink into the welcome blackness where pain was obliterated, but she could hear a voice and she forced her lashes up and stared dazedly at the man looming over her.

'Don't try to move. Lie still while I check to see if you've broken any bones. *Dios*—You are lucky you are still alive,' the voice said roughly. 'You flew through the air like a rag doll.'

Rachel was vaguely aware of hands running over her body, working up from her legs to her hips and then skimming her ribcage and, despite the lightness of the man's touch, she winced when he found the tender area on her lower rib. Still stunned by the fall, her lashes drifted down again.

'Hey, don't pass out. I'm going to call an ambulance.'

'I don't need an ambulance,' she muttered fiercely, forcing her eyes open again. The blackness was disappearing and above her she could see the blue sky dotted with wisps of cotton wool clouds. But then the stranger leaned over her, his face so close to hers that she could feel his warm breath graze her cheek, and for a moment she wondered if she was concussed—or hallucinating.

She recognised him instantly. Diego Ortega—international polo champion, multimillionaire and playboy who, according to the press, was as successful in his pursuit of beautiful women as he was of polo titles. Rachel had no interest in gossip columns, but since she was twelve years old she had devoured every riding magazine she could lay her hands on and there was no doubt that the Argentinian was a legend in his chosen sport.

She supposed she should not be surprised by his sudden appearance when, for the past few weeks, the main topic of conversation among the other stable-hands had been his impending visit to Hardwick Hall. But seeing him in the flesh was still a shock, and the realisation that he had been watching her take Piran over the jumps was disconcerting.

He had already extracted his mobile phone from his jeans. Rachel forced herself to sit up, biting down on her lip to stop herself from crying out as her battered body protested.

'I told you to lie still.' Diego Ortega's heavily accented voice was terse with a mixture of concern and impatience.

She instinctively rebelled against his authoritative tone. 'And I told you I don't need an ambulance,' she replied firmly as she curled her legs and managed by sheer determination to get onto her knees.

'Are you always so disobedient?' Diego made no effort to disguise his irritation and muttered something in his native tongue, in a tone that made Rachel glad that she could not understand Spanish. Once she was on her feet she would feel better, she told herself. She certainly didn't have a couple of hours to waste sitting in the waiting room at the local hospital. Gritting her teeth, she forced herself to move, and then gave a yelp of surprise when strong, tanned hands settled around her waist and she was lifted into the air.

She could not have been held against Diego Ortega's muscular chest for more than a second, but the feel of his powerful arms around her and the tantalising waft of his cologne that assailed her senses made her head swim. Her heart was beating too fast, and it was no good trying to kid herself that its accelerated speed was a result of the fall. Up close, he was awesome. Her eyes strayed to his broad chest where his casual cream shirt was open at the throat, revealing dark hairs that she noticed also covered his forearms. Slowly she lifted her head and studied his square jaw, the sharply chiselled cheekbones and wide mouth with its perfectly curved upper lip.

What would it be like to be kissed by that mouth? The thought hurtled uninvited into her mind and the blood that had drained from her cheeks due to the shock of the fall now flooded back, scalding her skin. Her gaze skittered over his face and clashed with amber eyes that at this moment were glinting warningly beneath heavy black brows.

His eyes had the golden hue of sherry, Rachel noted distractedly, desperately trying to hide the fact that her legs were wobbling when he set her on her feet. She was bound to feel peculiar after hurtling over Piran's head and meeting the ground at speed. The shaky feeling had nothing to do with the man who was looming over her, she told herself as her eyes strayed to his gleaming mahogany-coloured hair which fell to his shoulders.

His rugged good-looks were entirely masculine, and with his olive-gold skin he reminded her of a picture she'd once seen of a Sioux chief—dark, dangerous and undeniably the sexiest man she had ever laid eyes on.

He was still gripping her arms, as if he feared she would topple over if he let her go. He was too close, too big and way too overwhelming, and she needed to put some space between them.

'Thanks,' she murmured as she stepped back from him.

For a moment it seemed as though he would not release her, but then he took his hands from her arms, his eyes narrowing when she swayed unsteadily.

'You need to see a medic,' he said tersely. 'Even though you're wearing a hard hat, you could be suffering from concussion.'

'I'm fine, honestly,' Rachel assured him quickly, forcing a smile and trying to ignore the feeling that she'd been run over by a steamroller. 'I've had far worse falls than that.'

'I'm not surprised,' Diego growled. 'The horse is too big for you.' His mouth compressed as he relived those gut-churning seconds when the horse had refused the jump and its rider had been flung through the air, to land in a crumpled heap on the hard ground.

He turned his head and cast an expert eye over the black stallion which had first captured his attention when he had strolled down to the practice paddock. His interest in the rider had come afterwards, when the braid of golden hair hanging beneath the riding hat had told him that the boyishly slim figure astride the horse was in fact most definitely female.

The horse was easily seventeen hands, Diego estimated. It seemed calm now that the noise of the motorbike had faded but it was clearly a nervy creature and its highly strung nature, teamed with its physical size and strength, would make it a difficult animal for a man to control, let alone the slender woman standing before him.

She was startlingly beautiful, he acknowledged, feeling a tug of interest as he studied her small heart-shaped face. Her skin was bare of make-up and porcelain smooth, her cheeks flushed like rosy apples from her exertions over the jumps. She was a true English rose, and he was captivated by her cornflower-blue eyes, which were regarding him steadily from beneath the brim of her riding hat.

Diego frowned, astonished by the sudden realisation that he was staring at her. He was used to women staring at *him*— with varying degrees of subtlety and frequently a blatant invitation in their glances, which he responded to when he felt like it. Never had he been so fixated by a woman that he could not take his eyes off her. But this woman was simply exquisite—and so fragile looking that he was amazed she had not broken every bone in her body in the fall.

Riding the big stallion was plain folly, he brooded. 'I'm amazed your father allows you to ride such a powerful animal.'

'My father?' Nonplussed, Rachel stared at him. Neither her real father nor her mother's two subsequent husbands, who she had insisted that Rachel call 'Dad', had ever been sufficiently interested in her to care what sort of animal she rode. But Diego Ortega knew nothing of her complicated family, or the fact that her mother was a serial bride, and she frowned as she focused on the word *'allow'*.

'Neither my father nor anyone else "allows" me to do anything,' she said sharply. 'I'm an adult, and I make my own decisions. And I am more than capable of handling Piran.'

'He's too strong for you, and you're a fool to think you could control him if he decided to bolt,' Diego replied coolly.

'You plainly couldn't control him when he refused the jump—although, to be fair, that was not entirely your fault. Who the hell was that on the motorbike? I can't believe Earl Hardwick is happy for a yob to tear around the estate like a lunatic.'

'Unfortunately, the Earl allows his son to do whatever he likes,' Rachel said tersely, still incensed by Diego's remarks that she could not control Piran. 'The *yob* you're referring to was Jasper Hardwick, and I couldn't agree more with your description of him. He spends much of his time carving up the fields on his wretched bike. He shot out of the woods without warning, and it was no wonder Piran was startled. I'd challenge any rider to have been able to handle him in that situation.'

'Perhaps so,' Diego admitted with a shrug. 'You ride well,' he acknowledged grudgingly. When he had first arrived at the paddock he'd witnessed the empathy between the girl and the horse—that instinctive understanding that could not be taught or bought but was so vital in whichever competitive arena you were in. The girl was fearless in the saddle. There had been absolutely no hesitation when she had approached the six-foot jump and, although Diego had given up showjumping in favour of polo in his late teens, he knew enough about the sport to recognise her undoubted talent.

He walked over to the stallion, now standing patiently by the fence, and took hold of his reins. 'How old is he?' he queried, running his hand over the animal's flank.

'Six—I've been jumping him for two years.'

'He's a fine animal. What did you say you call him?'

'Piran. He comes from a stud in Cornwall, and his name means "dark"—rather appropriate for his colouring,' Rachel said softly, running her fingers through Piran's jet-black mane at the same time as Diego reached out to stroke the horse. His hand brushed against hers and she caught her breath at the brief touch of his warm skin, and then blushed furiously at the sudden gleam in his eyes that told her he had noticed her reaction to him.

His voice was so gravelly that it seemed to rumble from deep in his massive chest as he spoke again. 'So…the horse is Piran…and his rider is…?'

'Rachel Summers,' she answered briskly. She was head groom at Hardwick Polo Club, and it was likely that she would be in charge of Diego's horses at the upcoming polo match, where he would be the star guest. She wanted him to think she was a professional and experienced stable-hand, not a simpering idiot. She unfastened the strap under her chin and removed her riding hat. 'And you are Diego Ortega,' she said politely. 'Everyone here at Hardwick is excited about your visit, Mr Ortega.'

Dark eyebrows winged upwards and Rachel cringed. Why hadn't she said *everyone has been looking forward to your visit* or *talking about your visit*—instead of using the word 'excited'? She sounded like a naïve teenager and Diego must have thought so too because he gave her an amused smile.

'In the same way that the meaning of Piran suits your horse's colouring, I see that your name matches the shade of your hair. It is the colour of ripened wheat in mid-summer, Miss Summers,' he murmured, his eyes drawn to the wisps of gold curls that framed her face and the long braid that had slipped forwards over one shoulder. She was tiny—probably not more than a couple of inches over five feet tall—and when he had lifted her in his arms she had weighed next to nothing. Remarkably, she seemed relatively unscathed by her fall, although he could tell she was in pain around her ribs. But, despite her delicate appearance, she was as feisty and spirited as one of the prize colts from his stud at the Estancia Elvira, back home in Argentina.

'You look as though you are barely out of high school,' he drawled, his mouth twitching when she glared at him. 'How old are you?' he asked her.

'Twenty-two,' Rachel snapped, drawing herself up and wishing heartily that she was six inches taller. She knew she looked younger than her age and, as she rarely bothered to spend more time on her appearance than it took to wash her face and braid her hair, she accepted that it was her own fault Diego Ortega had probably mistaken her for a teenager. She did not care about his opinion of her looks, she told herself irritably, but she was proud of her riding skills and she was incensed that he had questioned her ability to control Piran.

She was breathing hard, her chest lifting and falling erratically, and she felt a jolt of shock when Diego's dark eyes trailed slowly over her body and focused deliberately on her breasts. Rachel swallowed and reminded herself that there was nothing much beneath her shirt to excite him. Riding was more than just her passion—since she was a teenager it had been an obsession that exceeded any vague interest in her appearance, and it had never bothered her that she had failed to develop a big bust. Now, for the first time in her life, she wished she looked more feminine and possessed curves rather than boyishly slender hips and a couple of minuscule bumps that did not require the support of a bra.

Diego's gaze caused the tiny hairs on Rachel's body to stand on end. Her legs suddenly felt weak and her breath seemed to be trapped in her chest—the same feeling she'd experienced a few moments ago when Piran had thrown her and she had struggled to her feet—winded and wobbly and strangely light-headed.

During her adolescence she had been so busy with her riding that she'd had no time for boys, and although she'd had a couple of relationships since she had left school they had quickly petered out through a lack of interest on her part. Diego Ortega was nothing like the men she had dated—and he was looking at her in a way that no man had ever done before. Her experience of the opposite sex might be limited, but she sensed Diego's interest. Some primal instinct inside her recognised the chemistry between them, and she could not restrain the little shiver of awareness that ran down her spine.

Diego's eyes narrowed. Rachel wasn't wearing a bra—he could clearly make out the darker flesh of her nipples—and as he watched they hardened into tight little peaks that jutted provocatively towards him. Heat surged through him, shocking him with its intensity. He hadn't felt this aroused for years. He did not understand why he was so acutely aware of her but, to his intense irritation, his heart was pounding and his jeans suddenly felt uncomfortably tight.

It was time for him to move, to break out of the sensual web that entrapped them both. A glance at his watch warned him that he should return to the Hall and change in time for dinner with the Earl and Lady Hardwick and their attractive but tediously overeager daughter, Felicity. He wondered if the idiot son who had nearly caused a serious accident would be present. He certainly intended to inform the Earl that he would not permit noisy motorbikes to be ridden near to the thoroughbred polo ponies he had been invited to Hardwick Polo Club to train.

His eyes strayed back to Rachel Summers's face and focused on her soft mouth, his stomach clenching when he imagined crushing those moist lips beneath his and exploring her with his tongue. She would taste as sweet as a light summer wine, and she would respond to him willingly—he noted how her eyes were now the colour of wood-smoke, her pupils dilated with sensual promise.

She could prove an interesting diversion over the next couple of months, he mused idly. He wondered who she was. He knew that the aristocratic Hardwick family had many off-shoots, and he assumed that Rachel must be a relative.

'Are you staying up at the Hall?' he demanded abruptly, forcing himself to step away from her.

'Earl Hardwick isn't in the habit of inviting his stable-hands to live in,' Rachel replied dryly. 'Not even his head groom.'

'So you work here.' Diego frowned. 'Do you own Piran?' He knew that most yards paid low wages, but the stallion was a thoroughbred and must have cost several thousand pounds.

'No, I have him on loan. His owner is Peter Irving, from the farm adjoining the Hardwick estate. Peter used to be a world-class showjumper, and he's my sponsor.'

'Irving—the name is familiar.'

'Three times Olympic gold medallist and top rider with the British Equestrian team for many years. Peter is my inspiration,' Rachel explained.

Diego caught the note of fierce determination in her voice and glanced at her curiously. 'You hope to be selected for the British team?'

'The next Olympics are my dream,' Rachel admitted, blushing and wondering why on earth she had revealed her life's ambition to a man she had never met before. She had never told anyone, apart from Peter Irving, of her hopes of competing at the highest level—not her friends, and certainly not her family. Since her parents had divorced when she was nine, they had both been too wrapped up in their lives with their new partners and children to take much interest in her, and the few times she had mentioned her riding to her mother it had led to the old argument about getting a proper job, somewhere decent to live rather than an old caravan, and a boyfriend.

'The Olympics are a long way off,' she murmured. 'For now I'm working hard in the hope of being picked for the team for the European championships next year. Peter and Earl Hardwick both think I have a good chance. The Earl has been very supportive of my career,' she added. 'He allows me to stable Piran here, and he always gives me time off to go to competitions. The facilities at Hardwick are excellent, and working here is a fantastic experience.'

'But not quite so fantastic when your horse refuses a jump,' Diego said dryly, his sharp gaze noting how she had crossed her arms over her chest and was surreptitiously rubbing her ribs. 'I'll ride Piran back to the stables for you.'

Without giving Rachel time to argue, he deftly adjusted the stirrups and swung into the saddle with a lithe grace and expertise. Piran did not usually take to strangers but, to Rachel's annoyance, he stood as docile as a lamb while Diego spoke to him in Spanish. The deep-timbred voice was strangely hypnotic; Piran's ears pricked up and he whinnied—almost as if he were talking back, although that was just fanciful imagination, Rachel told herself irritably. It was a pity that the Argentinian horseman did not have such a soothing effect on her. She felt decidedly rattled, and she knew it was not only because of the fall.

She opened the paddock gate and Diego took Piran through, but then halted and waited for her. 'I still think I should call a doctor,' he said, his mouth thinning when he noted how she winced with every step she took. 'You're as pale as a ghost and clearly in agony.'

'I'm just bruised, that's all,' Rachel argued stubbornly.

Diego gave her a hard stare. 'You're going to be black and blue and you'll ache tomorrow. To be on the safe side, you shouldn't ride for the next week.'

'Are you kidding?' Rachel looked scandalised. 'I've got a competition coming up and I'm going to take Piran round the course again tomorrow. He'd have managed that last fence fine if he hadn't been startled by the bike.'

Diego let out a curse, torn between impatience and admiration at her mulish determination. 'You are the most argumentative woman I have ever met, Miss Summers.' He moved before Rachel could guess his intention, and she gave a startled cry when he reached down and lifted her effortlessly onto Piran's back, placing her at the front of the saddle and clicking his tongue so that the horse immediately began to walk. One arm remained around her, holding her against his chest, while he held the reins in his other hand and controlled the stallion with impressive ease.

Attempting to scramble down would be futile, Rachel acknowledged as she stared at Diego's muscular forearms. She would just have to sit still until they reached the stable block, but she absolutely would not give in to the temptation to relax and lean her head against his chest. He was too close as it was, and the feel of his hard thighs pressing against her bottom seemed shockingly intimate. She was agonisingly aware of him—of the heat that emanated from him and the sensual musk of his cologne mixed with another subtle scent that was excitingly male and utterly intoxicating.

She was thankful when they reached the yard. Diego dismounted first and then carefully lifted her down. He seemed to think she was the rag doll he had described when he had witnessed her flying out of the saddle, she thought irritably as he strode into the barn, still holding her in his arms. His heart was beating steadily beneath her ear, but hers was thudding erratically and she was supremely conscious of his hands holding her beneath her knees and around the upper part of her body so that his fingers brushed lightly against the side of her breast.

She was pink-cheeked when he sat her down on a hay bale, and she glared at him when he leaned over her to prevent her from jumping to her feet. 'I need to see to Piran,' she said angrily.

'I'll ask one of the other grooms to rub him down. Every breath you take is agony—I can see it in your eyes, even if you are too stubborn to admit it,' Diego said grimly.

Rachel stared at his hard-boned face and it slowly dawned on her that she had finally met someone whose determination to have his own way matched her own. 'I've told you I'm fine,' she muttered. 'And Piran doesn't like anyone else to groom him.'

'Well, he's going to have to get used to it because I don't want to see you around these stables until you've had your ribs X-rayed and been thoroughly checked over by a doctor. My chauffeur, Arturo, will drive you to the hospital,' Diego informed her coolly. 'I would take you myself, but Lady Hardwick is giving a dinner party this evening—and I believe I'm the star guest,' he added dryly.

'Don't waste your breath arguing with me, Miss Summers,'

he warned, placing his finger beneath her chin and exerting gentle pressure so that she had no option but to shut her mouth and swallow the angry words that were bursting to escape. 'I will be in charge of the stables for the duration of my stay at Hardwick Hall, and I refuse to have anyone working here who can't pull their weight. If you've broken your ribs, or sustained other injuries today, you'll be a liability I can do without.'

Unfazed by her furious expression, he smiled, revealing his gleaming white teeth that contrasted with his bronzed skin. 'I can't keep on calling you Miss Summers all summer—can I, Rachel?'

His voice had altered, and was now as thick and sensuous as molten honey, but Rachel was determined not to be impressed. Clearly he was an outrageous flirt, as well as the most arrogant man she had ever met, and she was furious with her treacherous body for responding to him. She was aware of a tingling sensation in her breasts and a shocking yearning for him to push her down into the hay, lower himself onto her and kiss her like she had never been kissed before.

'What do you mean by "all summer"?' she croaked. 'I know you're here for the polo tournament, but surely you'll be going back to Argentina straight afterwards.'

Diego shook his head, his smile widening at Rachel's look of dismay. 'As a matter of fact, I usually spend a couple of months—when it is winter in Argentina—at my polo school just outside New York. But this year the Earl has invited me to Hardwick to train the polo ponies.

'So you see, Rachel,' he drawled softly, moving his finger from under her chin and gently tracing the shape of her lips with his thumb pad, 'for the next month or so I will be your boss, and you will have to abide by my rules. Go to the hospital with Arturo, get yourself checked over, and when you can come back to me with a clean bill of health you will be welcome here. Until then, if I catch so much as a strand of your pretty blonde hair near Piran's loose box, there will be trouble. *Entiendes?*'

There was a hint of steel behind his mocking tone that warned Rachel he would be a dangerous man to cross. Incensed by his high-handedness, she jerked her head away, disgusted to find that she was trembling. The feather-light caress of his thumb over her lips had been shockingly intimate, and the idea that she would be working for him over the summer was downright disturbing.

'Earl Hardwick personally appointed me as head groom, and I'm sure he'll have something to say when I tell him you've banned me from doing my job,' she said furiously.

'The Earl had a hard job persuading me to come to Gloucestershire rather than New York, and I think you'll find that he'll go along with anything *I* say,' Diego replied with a breathtaking arrogance that made Rachel itch to slap him. 'Besides, you are not banned, Rachel. I am very much looking forward to working with you once I am assured that you suffered no serious injuries today. I have great plans for Hardwick Polo Club, and I have a feeling that you and I will be spending a lot of time together.'

The sensuous gleam in his eyes was unmistakable, and a quiver ran down Rachel's spine. She wanted to jump up and tell him to get lost—tell him that she'd rather work for the devil than him. But she couldn't move. For one thing, her ribs were seriously painful—but the real reason, she acknowledged dismally, was that she was trapped by his magnetism and utterly captivated by his raw masculinity. He was the most potently virile man she had ever met; she could not tear her eyes from his sensual mouth and when he lowered his head slowly towards her, she ceased thinking, almost ceased breathing, her heart hammering with frantic excitement when it seemed that he was going to kiss her.

To her intense disappointment, he did not. Instead, he straightened up abruptly and moved away from her, giving her a mocking smile that added to her humiliation.

'Wait here for Arturo,' he ordered. He strode across the barn and halted in the doorway to glance back at her. 'It promises to be an interesting summer, don't you think, Rachel?' he taunted softly.

CHAPTER TWO

TO RACHEL'S relief an X-ray showed that she had not broken any bones when Piran had thrown her, but her ribs and shoulder were badly bruised and the doctor was adamant that she should not ride for a few days.

'I doubt you'll be able to move tomorrow,' he told her as he handed her a prescription for strong painkillers. 'Take two of these twice a day, and if I were you I'd go to bed and stay there.'

It was the most ridiculous suggestion Rachel had ever heard. She had never spent a day in bed in her life, and as far as she was concerned the fact that she hadn't suffered any fractures meant that she would be fit to work at the stables tomorrow.

But the following morning she woke in agony and the sight of her purple bruises forced her to accept that she was in no fit state to ride her bicycle up to the stables, muck out loose boxes and then spend the morning exercising the horses.

Besides, even if she managed to get to the stables, Diego Ortega was likely to send her straight home again. The Argentinian was the most arrogant individual she had ever met. Infuriatingly, he was also the sexiest man she had ever laid eyes on, she acknowledged grimly. She cringed when she remembered how she had been so mesmerised by him that she had stared at him, hoping he would kiss her, and his amused smile had told her that he had known exactly what she was thinking.

The day dragged endlessly, but fortunately the painkillers worked well and by early evening Rachel was feeling less like she had been trampled on by a herd of bulls and was bored of her enforced isolation. One of the other stable-hands sent her a text saying that Diego had returned to the Hall, where he was staying as a guest of Earl Hardwick. He was unlikely to visit the stables again tonight, Rachel decided as she cycled through the woods to the Hardwick estate, wincing every time she hit a pothole on the path.

Piran was gratifyingly pleased to see her. From his gleaming coat she guessed that someone must have groomed him, but she gave him another brush and fed him a couple of peppermints, and did not notice she had company until a figure came up silently behind her.

'Jasper, you'll give me a heart attack if you creep up on me like that,' she snapped when a faint sound made her swing round and she almost collided with Earl Hardwick's son and heir. 'It's a pity you weren't so quiet on your bike yesterday,' she muttered, feeling the same uneasy tension that always gripped her when she was alone with Jasper. The young Englishman was reputedly one of the most eligible bachelors among the landed gentry and, with his blonde hair flopping onto his brow, Rachel could see why women might be attracted to him. But he did nothing for her, and she hated the way he looked at her as though he were mentally undressing her.

'Yeah, I heard Piran threw you when you were jumping him yesterday.' Jasper lounged in the stable doorway, blocking Rachel's path so that she instinctively stepped backwards away from him.

'It was your fault, not his. The noise of your bike scared him. I wish you wouldn't ride it near the paddock.'

Jasper gave a careless shrug. 'It's my land—or it will be one day. You know, it would pay you to be nice to me, Rachel,' he said with a sly smile, reaching out and running his finger down her cheek. 'One day I'm going to be very rich—as long as my dear papa doesn't blow the family fortune on the polo club. God knows how much he's had to fork out to persuade Diego Ortega to come here and share his "expertise",' he added petulantly. 'Ortega is already a multimillionaire, and the money the old man's paying him could have gone on increas-. ing my paltry allowance.'

'Mr Ortega is reputed to be one of the best trainers in the world,' Rachel murmured. 'And his appearance at the Hardwick Polo Tournament has trebled ticket sales, which must be good for the club.'

'Ortega is a notorious playboy,' Jasper said sulkily, clearly resenting Rachel's defence of him. And why *had* she spoken up for Diego when the first thing he had done since his arrival had been to ban her from the stables? she wondered irritably. 'My sister was all over him like a rash at dinner last night,' Jasper added sneeringly. 'Don't tell me you've fallen for his smarmy charm too?'

'Of course not,' she replied quickly; perhaps too quickly because Jasper stared at her intently and she felt herself blush. She could not bear for Jasper of all people to guess the effect that Diego had on her and so she added, 'From my brief meeting with Diego Ortega, I found him to be the most objectionable man I've ever met and, like you, I'll be glad to see the back of him.'

'Is that so, Rachel? How disappointing. I had such high hopes for our relationship,' a familiar, heavily accented voice drawled mockingly behind her. Rachel gasped and jerked her head round to see Diego strolling in through the doors of the stable block. 'Our working relationship, of course,' he added, giving Jasper Hardwick a bland smile when the young Englishman glowered at him.

Diego turned his attention back to Rachel, and she felt a fluttering sensation in her stomach as her eyes clashed with his gleaming amber gaze. He had obviously changed for dinner and looked stunningly handsome in tailored black trousers and a white silk shirt. Presumably he would don a tuxedo and bow tie before dinner with the Hardwicks, but for now his shirt was open at the throat, revealing his golden skin.

'I'm afraid you'll be seeing a lot of me over the next few weeks—back and front,' he said sarcastically, while she stared at the floor and wished a trapdoor would miraculously open beneath her feet. 'Earl Hardwick has challenged me to turn Hardwick Polo Club into a top sporting venue—and I can never resist a challenge,' he murmured silkily, his eyes focused on Rachel's flushed face.

He glanced dismissively at Jasper. 'I'm afraid you will no longer be able to ride your motorbike around the estate. I'll be doing some intensive training with the polo ponies and I don't want to waste my time calming them down after you've terrified them. Your thoughtless actions yesterday caused Rachel's accident, and it was sheer luck the outcome wasn't more serious.'

An angry flush stained Jasper's face. 'It's not my fault Rachel can't control her horse,' he said sullenly. 'Everyone knows Piran is too strong for her.' He gave Diego a look of active dislike. 'You can't tell me what to do. My father…'

'Your father agrees with me that the bike should be banned from anywhere near the stables and practice paddocks,' Diego interrupted with a quiet authority in his tone that brought another wave of colour to Jasper's face. 'Miss Summers's riding skills are not in question. I was watching her yesterday, and in my opinion she is an excellent horsewoman.'

Rachel blushed at the unexpected praise. Jasper glanced furiously from her to Diego and swore viciously before he swung round and stormed out of the stables. In the silence that fell after his departure Rachel felt her tension rise and she busied herself with putting Piran's grooming brushes away.

'He may be a member of the British aristocracy but he's a charmless individual, isn't he?' Diego drawled. 'But perhaps you don't think so, Rachel? Did you arrange to meet Hardwick here, when you knew the other grooms would have finished work and the two of you would be alone?'

Stunned by the accusation, she spun round and saw that his amber eyes were coldly assessing her. 'Of course not,' she denied sharply. 'Why would I? I'm not the slightest bit interested in Jasper.'

Diego stepped into the loose box and patted Piran. 'Well, he's interested in you,' he said harshly. 'A word of advice, *querida*—don't flirt with Hardwick unless you intend to follow it through. He wants you badly, and it's not a good idea to lead him on.'

'I wasn't *flirting* with him!' Rachel's eyes flashed with temper. 'He must have seen me arrive here and followed me into the stables.' She trailed to a halt, remembering how Diego had expressly banned her from visiting the stables. 'I came to see Piran, not to ride him,' she muttered and then, as her temper sparked again, added, 'although the X-rays were clear. I didn't break any bones yesterday, and there's no reason why I can't ride.'

'Apart from the doctor's recommendation that you take a break from riding for a few days—Arturo overheard your conversation at the hospital,' Diego murmured dryly, feeling a mixture of amusement and impatience when she glared at him. She was infuriatingly stubborn—a trait they shared, he acknowledged. He understood her obsession for riding and her addiction to the adrenalin boost when she took her horse over the jumps. She clearly pushed herself to the limits, just as he did on the polo field, but he wondered what demons drove her and made her careless of her safety—as his demons drove him to take risks which had taken him to the top of his sport, and on several occasions within a whisker of the grave.

He was torn between wanting to shake some sense into her and kiss the mutinous line of her mouth until she parted her lips and allowed him to push his tongue between them. He was irritated by the effect she had on him. Yesterday he had thought she would be an interesting diversion while he was staying at Hardwick, but after spending a restless night when he'd been unable to dismiss her from his mind he had decided that she was a complication he could do without. He had confidently assumed that when he saw her again he would have his inconvenient attraction to her under control, but as soon as he'd walked into the stables and felt his heart jolt at the sight of her he had been forced to admit that his awareness of her had not lessened.

Her hair was the colour of spun gold, falling to halfway down her back. He wanted to run his fingers through the thick, silky mass and then pull her into his arms so that her hips cradled the hard evidence of his arousal. His body was as taut as an over-strung bow and he felt an overwhelming urge to tumble her down in the hay, but instead he called on all his willpower and stepped out of Piran's loose box.

'As you can see, Piran is fine, and he gave me no trouble when I groomed him earlier.' He followed Rachel out of the loose box. 'I'll drive you home. I understand you live at Irving's farm.'

'Yes, but there's no need for you to give me a lift—I cycled here.' Rachel nodded towards her bike, propped up against the barn wall. 'It's quicker for me to ride through the woods.'

'I want to discuss the horses I've brought over from Argentina for the polo tournament. If you are going to oppose everything I say, I will have to seriously question whether I can have you working here,' Diego snapped.

Was he threatening to sack her? Rachel chewed on her lip as panic surged through her. How could she admit that her reluctance to sit next to him in the close confines of the sleek silver sports car she could see parked in the yard was due to her acute awareness of him? But he gave her no further opportunity to speak and was already striding out of the barn. She hurried after him and when he held open the car door she slid into the passenger seat and stared determinedly ahead, her senses flaring when he sat behind the wheel and she inhaled the exotic scent of his aftershave.

'You were going to tell me about your horses,' she murmured tentatively when he had driven almost to the boundary of the Hardwick estate in a taut silence that played havoc with her nerves. Diego exhaled deeply, as if he too was aware of the prickling tension between them, but then proceeded to give her detailed information about his polo ponies. Rachel listened intently so that it was a surprise when the car came to a halt and she realised that they had turned into the farm.

'I've left notes about feeds and medical histories, et cetera in the tack room. You can read through them when you come back to work after the weekend,' he said in a tone that brooked no argument about when he would allow her back to the stables.

'Fine. Well, I'll see you next week then,' Rachel replied flatly, wondering how she was going to survive for three long days without riding. The prospect of not seeing Diego for days had nothing to do with the deflated feeling that had settled over her, she told herself firmly.

'Before you go…these are for you.' He reached behind his seat and handed her a huge bouquet of yellow roses, his mouth curving into a smile at her expression of stunned surprise. 'To wish you a speedy recovery,' he explained. 'When I visited the florist's the colour reminded me of your bright hair—and the sharp thorns were a painful reminder of your prickly nature,' he added dryly, showing her several deep scratches on his hand. 'I almost bled to death removing them.'

'I don't mean to be prickly; I'm just used to doing things for myself and making my own decisions, that's all,' Rachel mumbled, burying her face in the scented blooms because she could not bring herself to meet Diego's gaze. Unaccountably, her eyes filled with tears and she blinked fiercely to dispel them. She wondered what he would say if she revealed that she had never been given flowers in her life—and then wondered where on earth she was going to put them when she did not possess a vase.

She sensed he was waiting for her to say something, and forced herself to speak. 'They're beautiful. Thank you.'

'You're welcome.' Diego paused, and wondered impatiently why he felt as edgy as a teenager on a first date. Rachel was a stable-hand, with an attitude problem and a sharp tongue—not the sort of woman he would usually be interested in. But he was intrigued by her and as he watched her tongue dart out to moisten her lips the tug of desire that had kept him awake for half the night intensified. 'I was hoping they would persuade you to invite me in and offer me a cup of coffee.'

Rachel glanced at him, caught the unmistakable sensual gleam in his amber eyes and stared back at the golden bouquet, her heart beating very fast. It was only coffee, she reminded herself, and it seemed churlish to refuse when he had presented her with two dozen roses. 'You're welcome to come in for coffee. But I don't live at the farmhouse. I live up there.'

Following her gaze, Diego restarted the engine and drove up the track that wound out of the farmyard and through a small copse of trees, his brows lowering in a frown when the track ended at a small shabby caravan nestled in the shade of a towering oak tree. 'You don't seriously expect me to believe you live in *that*?'

'And the coffee is cheap instant,' Rachel said sweetly. 'Welcome to my home, Mr Ortega.' While Diego stared out of the windscreen in patent disbelief, she jumped out of the car and unlocked the caravan, the heat that had built up inside hitting her as she pushed open the door. He had probably changed his mind about the coffee, she decided, trying to ignore her disappointment as she rummaged around in the cupboard under the sink, searching for a suitable vessel to hold the roses. She had unearthed a couple of jam jars when he climbed up the steps, ducking his head as he stepped through the door and instantly seeming to dominate the cramped space.

He glanced around the interior of the caravan and Rachel

gave a silent groan when his eyes fell on the bed, which she had left down this morning because her shoulder had hurt too much to pack it away.

'It's what an estate agent might call a compact residence,' she said brightly. 'When the bed is folded away there's actually a surprising amount of room—for me, anyway,' she added when she glanced up and saw that Diego's head was brushing the ceiling.

'This can't be your permanent home.' He could not disguise his shock at her living conditions. 'You just camp out here during the summer—right?'

'No, I moved in here when I was seventeen, after my mother married for the third time and my twin half-sisters were born.'

Diego's brows rose. 'Family life sounds complicated.'

'Believe me, it is. I went to live with my father for a while, but he and his new wife had also just had a baby and it was easier for everyone when Peter Irving offered me the caravan.'

Rachel's voice was carefully controlled, giving no hint of how she had resented feeling like a spare part in her parents' lives—unwanted, apart from being an occasional babysitter to her various half brothers and sisters. She had spent most of her childhood being passed between her mother and father, but she often thought that the bitter custody battle they had fought over her had been more about them trying to score points off each other than because either of them had actually wanted her to live with them.

It had been a far from idyllic childhood, and by the age of twelve she had been fiercely independent—getting up early every morning to do a paper round to pay for her riding lessons. She preferred horses to people and, after witnessing her parents' various failed marriages, she was adamant that she never wanted to get married or be reliant on another human being.

'The caravan is sound and dry, although it does shake a bit

in strong wind,' Rachel admitted as she spooned coffee granules into the two least chipped mugs she could find. 'But it's got all the basic amenities—a shower, and Peter rigged up a generator to provide me with electricity. I can't afford to rent a house,' she explained when Diego gave her a look that said he seriously questioned her sanity. 'Property is very expensive around here, and everything I earn goes on Piran's upkeep and competition fees.'

Diego noted that the caravan might be small and old, but it was immaculately clean. The collection of china horses arranged on the shelf above the cooker were free from dust, and on the miniature kitchen worktop stood a jar filled with wild daisies. Rachel's home was as unconventional and dainty as its occupant, and he felt like a giant who had somehow squeezed himself into a doll's house.

He would drink the coffee and then leave, he decided, shaking his head when she offered milk and sugar, and grimacing when he took a sip of the foul black liquid she handed him. He didn't know why he hadn't simply dropped her off at the farm entrance.

His eyes strayed to her slender figure and her pert derrière, moulded by her jeans, and he felt a tightening sensation in his groin. He was used to dating sophisticated socialites who wouldn't be seen dead in anything other than designer labels, but there was something wholesome and incredibly sexy about Rachel's scrubbed face and simple clothes. He wondered if she was aware that the sunlight streaming in through the window made her shirt semi-transparent. He could clearly see the outline of her breasts, and liquid heat surged through his veins.

He took a gulp of the hot coffee and felt it scald the back of his throat. 'Do you live here alone?' he asked shortly.

Rachel glanced around the cramped living space, her brows lifting expressively. 'There's barely enough room for me, let alone anyone else,' she murmured.

'So, no boyfriend sharing your bunk?'

'No! I told you, I'm training hard in the hope of being picked for the British Equestrian team. I don't have time for boyfriends.' Much less the desire for one, she thought, her mouth firming. But that did not mean she was completely oblivious to men, or at least this man. She could not tear her eyes from Diego. He looked faintly incongruous, standing in her tiny caravan in his formal black trousers and beautifully tailored shirt. He reminded her of one of those impossibly gorgeous male models from a glossy magazine—and he should be somewhere exotic like Monte Carlo or Rio, not a field in rural Gloucestershire. But he *was* here, with her, and he was looking at her in a way that was making her heart race and her face feel hot.

She should have suggested that they drink their coffee outside, she thought frantically. But her garden furniture consisted of two upended feed buckets, and she could not picture suave Diego Ortega sprawling on the grass. The atmosphere inside the caravan suddenly seemed to be charged with electricity and she was agonisingly aware of his hard, lean body standing inches from her. She held her breath when he closed the gap between them, and her eyes darted nervously from his chest up to his face and focused helplessly on his sensual mouth. Her heart seemed to stop beating when he slid his hand beneath her chin and lowered his face so close to hers that she could see the tiny lines that fanned out from the corners of his eyes.

'What…what do you think you're doing?' she demanded, dismayed that her voice sounded so weak and breathless when she wanted to give the impression that she was in complete control of the situation.

'I think I am going to kiss you,' Diego drawled, patently amused by the question. 'In fact, I know it, *querida*—just as I know that you want me to.'

Rachel's heart was jerking painfully beneath her ribs. 'I don't,' she said desperately, her cheeks flaming as she recalled how she had silently urged him to kiss her in the stables yesterday.

'Liar,' he said with gentle mockery which disguised the tension that gripped him. Her skin was almost translucent, her peaches-and-cream complexion as exquisite as a work of art, and her mouth, pink and moist and slightly parted, was a temptation he could no longer resist. The sexual awareness between them was white-hot—and mutual. Rachel might try to deny it, but her eyes were huge with excitement, the invitation in their depths unmistakable. He hesitated for a second, wanting to savour the anticipation, but as he brushed his lips over hers in that first explorative caress and felt her tentative response, hunger coursed through his veins and with a muffled groan he crushed her mouth beneath his and kissed her with unrestrained passion.

It did not cross Rachel's mind to resist him—and, even if her brain clung to some last vestige of sanity, her body had a will of its own and demanded her complete and utter surrender. Diego's lips were warm and firm, sliding over hers with such erotic skill that she simply melted against him and opened her mouth, her heart thudding in her chest at the first bold thrust of his tongue.

Nothing in her life had prepared her for the storm of sensations that swept through her. She had never experienced true desire before; not this desperate need for something she did not even understand but which raged inside her as wild and dangerous as a bush fire.

Perhaps her subconscious mind had deliberately subdued her normal sexual urges? she wondered vaguely, finding it hard to think straight when Diego slid his arms around her and drew her against the hard wall of his chest.

But now those urges had been awakened, and she could not control them. The pressure of his mouth on hers was as addictive as a drug, and she wanted more. She placed her hands on his chest and felt the heat of his body through his silk shirt. What would it be like to feel his bare skin pressed against hers?

But, before she could give in to her heated fantasy, Diego suddenly dropped down so that he was sitting on the edge of her makeshift bed and pulled her onto his lap.

'That's better, hmm…?' he murmured against her mouth, before he kissed her again, moving his lips on hers with undisguised passion which sent a shiver of need down her spine. She was trembling, every nerve-ending tingling, and when he brushed his hand lightly over her breast she shivered in anticipation of a more intimate caress.

'Do you like that, *querida*?' His voice was a husky growl, but Rachel was beyond giving an answer, the feelings he was arousing in her were new and wondrous and she was swept away to a place where nothing mattered except that Diego should continue to kiss her and touch her. She heard him mutter something in his own language, and was vaguely aware of his fingers gently stroking her waist before inching up towards her ribs once more. The bright sunlight streaming through the window made her squint, and through her half closed eyes he seemed dark and forbidding—a stranger who had kissed her until she could not think straight.

As he gently increased the pressure of his caresses, Rachel suddenly drew in a sharp breath. Aware that her rapid intake of air had nothing to do with arousal, Diego quickly removed his hands before he gently pushed her shirt over her shoulder, revealing the fragile line of her collarbone—and the mass of purple bruises that contrasted starkly with her pale skin.

'Your injuries are worse even than I imagined,' he said harshly, the sound of his voice shattering the last of the sexual haze that had held Rachel a willing prisoner in his arms. The fire in her veins cooled as quickly as if he had thrust her beneath an ice-cold shower, leaving her feeling slightly sick. What had she been thinking, allowing a man she barely knew to kiss her, and touch her…?

Diego was staring at her bony shoulder with a look of undisguised horror, and she felt embarrassed that he was clearly repelled by her body. With a jerky movement that jolted her ribs and caused her to wince in pain, she snatched the edges of her shirt together to hide the offending bruises from his gaze. 'I'd like you to leave,' she said tightly. 'You've had your fun.'

'My fun?' Diego stiffened, his eyes narrowing on her flushed face.

Rachel was aware that she sounded abrupt to the point of rudeness, but she was dying of mortification as she recalled her wanton response to him. What must he think of her? She had made no attempt to stop him kissing her. The moment he had taken her in his arms, she had melted against him and kissed him back; and her soft moans of pleasure when he had caressed her must have sent out a message that she was his for the taking.

Since she was old enough to understand adult relationships, she had proudly announced that she would never act like her mother, lurching blindly between marriages and affairs with no thought to the consequences. She would never allow any man that kind of power over her, she'd stated confidently. Yet here she was, practically making love with a stranger just because he was the most gorgeous male she'd ever met.

'I don't know what you were expecting,' she snapped, taking her anger with herself out on him, 'but I am not the kind of woman who jumps into bed with a man five minutes after meeting him.'

'You could have fooled me,' Diego drawled, the warmth that had blazed in his amber eyes turning rapidly to an expression of icy arrogance. 'I was not expecting anything,' he snapped, furious with himself that he had come on to her like some callow youth. It was not his style. He always played it cool with women, and he had meant to stop after one brief kiss. Rachel's passionate response had blown him away, but he wasn't prepared to take all the blame. 'Do you seriously expect me to believe that if I hadn't stopped just then, you would have called a halt?' He gave a disbelieving laugh that sparked Rachel's temper. 'Don't kid yourself, Rachel. Your need was as great as mine—and still is,' he said coolly as he trailed his hand insolently down the front of her shirt and noted how her nipples jutted to attention.

He watched her cheeks flood with colour, and with an impatient movement he stood up and strode over to the door of the caravan, snatching oxygen into his lungs as he stared over the lush green English countryside. He was only going to be here for a few weeks, and he had a job to do that promised to be interesting. Rachel played an important role at Hardwick. He had learned from talking to the other grooms that she was highly regarded for her dedication to the horses and the polo club, and he needed to establish a good working relationship with her. The attraction between them was seriously inconvenient—but if Rachel could fight it then so could he.

'This was a mistake,' she said huskily. For some reason the discernible tremor in her voice tugged at Diego's insides. He turned his head and saw that she had buttoned her shirt right up to the neck. 'I wasn't expecting you to kiss me…and I admit I got carried away. I can't believe I fell for the "can I come in for coffee?" line,' she choked. Her eyes fell on the glorious yellow roses and she felt sick. 'Is that what the flowers were for—to soften me up for a quick sex session?'

'Of course not,' he grated, outraged at the accusation. She was making it sound as though she was some virginal innocent and he was an utter bastard who had cynically planned to seduce her, but neither was true. 'It was just a kiss,' he said coldly. 'I assure you I had no intention of asking you to jump into bed with me.'

It might have been 'just a kiss' to him, but for Rachel it had been the most devastatingly sensual experience of her life. Still, she would rather die than let him see how much he affected her, and she preferred to carry out a post-mortem of her behaviour away from his mocking gaze. 'Please go,' she said shakily. 'I think it would be best if we both forgot this…this…'

'Fascinating interlude?' Diego suggested sarcastically.

'Get out!' The glittering amusement in his eyes was the last straw and she clenched her fists and dared him—*dared* him—to say another word.

'I'm going.' He sauntered down the caravan steps and glanced back at her, his tone no longer mocking but quietly serious as he murmured, 'I agree we should try to forget the sexual chemistry that exists between us, Rachel. But I wonder if we can.'

CHAPTER THREE

THE heatwave, which had been unusual for early May, broke and on Monday morning Rachel walked up to the stables in the rain, dreading facing Diego again. Over the weekend she had come to the dismal conclusion that she had seriously overreacted. Of course he hadn't kissed her as a prelude to persuading her to sleep with him. He was a gorgeous playboy and a sporting hero who was frequently photographed in the tabloids in the company of beautiful models. He was hardly likely to have felt uncontrollable lust for a scruffy stable-girl.

His scathing dismissal of their kiss emphasised how unimportant he regarded the whole episode, but she had acted like a shocked virgin from a Victorian melodrama. No doubt that was because she was a shocked virgin, she acknowledged gloomily. Diego had made her feel things she had never felt before, and now she felt restless and unfulfilled.

She did not see him until later in the afternoon, when she and a few of the other grooms had been out exercising some of the polo ponies and gave them one last gallop back to the stables. Diego was wearing a knee-length black oilskin coat and matching wide-brimmed hat that shielded his face, but his height and the width of his shoulders made him instantly recognisable, and Rachel's heart lurched when she reined in her horse and they trotted into the yard.

'Are you sufficiently recovered from your accident to be

riding?' he greeted her as he strode over and caught hold of her pony's bridle.

'I'm fine,' she replied automatically, ignoring the nagging pain in her ribs. Her eyes were drawn to his mouth, and she blushed as she recalled the tingling pleasure of his kiss. She saw something flicker in his eyes and hastily looked away from him. 'I'd better go and rub Charlie Boy down. He's covered in mud.'

'You both are,' Diego said dryly. He did not understand how he could possibly be turned on by Rachel when she was wearing a bulky waxed jacket and mud-spattered jodhpurs. He usually liked women to look feminine and alluring—as if they'd spent their days in the beauty parlour and came to him beautifully groomed and coiffed and dressed in exquisite couture gowns. Rachel looked as though she had rolled in every muddy puddle she'd come across but, to his self-disgust, he imagined undressing her slowly, layer by layer, until he exposed her slender, pale body.

'How are the bruises?' he asked roughly.

'Fading,' she mumbled, remembering how he had unfastened her shirt and discovered the ugly purple marks on her shoulder, and how the desire in his eyes had rapidly disappeared. What would he make of her now that the bruises were turning an unattractive greenish yellow? She would never know, she told herself firmly. She was never going to allow him to touch her again, let alone undress her—and, from the cool expression in his eyes, he obviously regretted the whole episode as much as she did.

'You could have taken another day off,' he murmured. 'I can see that your shoulder is still stiff.'

'It's fine—and I'm not used to sitting around doing nothing. I'm not the world's most patient patient,' she owned honestly.

Amusement glinted in his eyes at her understatement. 'No, I don't suppose you are. When you've seen to your horse I'll give you a lift home. I have to go into the village and the farm is on my way.'

'Oh, no, it's okay—I'm not going home just yet.'

He frowned. 'There's nothing more to do here today.'

'I want to take Piran over the jumps,' Rachel admitted reluctantly.

He shook his head. 'That's not a good idea. It's your first day back and you must be tired.' He had watched her on several occasions during the day, when she had been unaware of him, and he was astounded at how hard she worked. She was so petite, and the life of a stable-hand was physically demanding, but from the moment she had arrived at the stables early this morning she had taken on more than her fair share of the workload.

If Rachel was honest, she was worn out and ached all over, but her innate stubbornness rebelled at Diego's dictatorial tone. 'Olympic champions don't get to the top of their sport by giving in every time they're tired,' she said briskly. 'Piran and I both need all the practice we can get before our next competition.'

'*Santa Madre!* You are the most headstrong, argumentative…' Diego inhaled deeply, trying to control his temper. 'I understand your desire to succeed as a showjumper, but it's sheer folly to take unnecessary risks.'

'Jumping is a dangerous sport—as is polo,' Rachel said tightly. 'How can you warn me about taking risks when your whole career has been built on the fact that you consistently risk your safety when you play? I've watched footage of you competing in tournaments, and you ride with a crazy disregard for your safety—almost as if you've got a death-wish,' she added, her voice faltering when the hard gleam in Diego's eyes warned her that she had gone too far.

'Don't be ridiculous,' he snapped coldly. 'I've been at the top of my sport for the past ten years and I know what I'm doing.'

Rachel shrugged. 'Fine—let's agree that I won't give you advice on your sport, and you won't tell me how to do mine.'

Diego glared at the mutinous line of her mouth and was

seriously tempted to kiss her into submission. She was as strong-willed and reckless as…as he had been at twenty-two, he owned grimly. She thought she was infallible, just as he had a decade ago, and he wanted to warn her that she wasn't— no one was.

Once he had been headstrong and impetuous, but it had been those traits that had caused his brother's death. Diego closed his eyes briefly, trying to stem the wave of pain that swept through him as he pictured Eduardo's lifeless body. Even after all this time the memories were agonising and the pain still raw. The ache in Diego's heart had never eased—nor had the belief that he had no right to experience happiness in his life when he had unwittingly caused Eduardo's accident.

Rachel was wrong about one thing; he brooded grimly as he watched her dismount and lead her pony into the stable. He did not have a death-wish—it was simply that his survival or otherwise was something that did not interest him unduly. He had spent the last ten years pushing himself to the limits and daring death to take him as it had taken his brother, and it was ironic that his recklessness had made him a national sporting hero in Argentina and a world renowned polo champion.

Hardwick Polo Tournament was always a popular event, but this year more tickets had been sold than usual because Diego Ortega would be playing for the home team. For the past two weeks Rachel had arrived at the stables at dawn and worked until dusk, helping to prepare the estate for the influx of twenty thousand visitors. Somehow she managed to fit in riding Piran. She'd felt apprehensive the first time she had taken him over the jumps after he had thrown her, and Diego's brooding presence at the edge of the paddock had only made things worse. But she forced herself to control her nerves— aware that Piran would pick up on her tension, and she was euphoric when he jumped the six foot fence with no problems.

She was less happy that Diego seemed to have appointed

himself as her minder and turned up without fail every evening when she took Piran down to the practice paddock. His presence unsettled her. *He* unsettled her; she admitted when she watched him stride into the yard on the morning of the polo tournament. He looked breathtakingly handsome in the Hardwick team colours—a gold shirt, taupe jodhpurs and black leather boots. As usual the sight of him made her pulse-rate quicken and she blushed when he looked over at her, the slight smile on his lips telling her that he was aware that she had been staring at him.

She had developed a monumental crush on him, she acknowledged ruefully, feeling a shiver of excitement run the length of her spine when his gaze lingered on her. She worked with him closely every day and was finding it increasingly hard to hide her attraction to him. And it was not just her physical awareness of him. Watching him train the polo ponies, she had been impressed by his skill and patience, and his amazing affinity with horses. He was an outstanding horseman, and she knew she could learn a lot from him. She wished she could relax and chat to him as easily as the other stable-hands did, but she felt tongue-tied whenever he spoke to her, and was terrified he would guess how much she longed for him to kiss her again.

Diego had been chatting with the other members of the Hardwick team, but now he detached himself from the group and walked over to collect the first of the four horses he would ride during the match. 'Do you have a partner to escort you to the after-tournament party, Rachel?' he queried casually as he swung himself into the saddle.

He hadn't yet donned his hard hat and in the sunlight his hair gleamed like raw silk on his shoulders, blown back from his face by the breeze. Rachel's heart jolted beneath her ribs and her voice emerged as a strangled sound. 'Alex asked me to go with him,' she mumbled. Alex was another groom and one of her closest friends. She saw Diego glance across the yard to where the copper-haired young man was leading out a polo pony, and he gave a slight shrug.

'What a pity. I was hoping I could persuade you to partner me tonight.' He gave her a bland smile, but the expression in his eyes stole her breath. It was gone before she could define it—yet she was sure she had not mistaken the look of feral hunger in his gaze, and she felt a surge of gut-churning disappointment that she had missed her chance to attend the party with him.

But what chance did she realistically have with Diego? she brooded later as she watched him tear around the polo pitch, controlling his horse with awesome skill. He dominated the field, and she doubted there was a woman present among the spectators who was not bowled over by his stunning looks and blatant virility.

At the end of the tournament he was presented with the winner's trophy by Felicity Hardwick, who looked pink cheeked and flustered as she gave him a congratulatory kiss. Afterwards he posed for photos with the promotional glamour models, and as Rachel stared at the bevy of beautiful blondes crowded around him, and then glanced down at her mud-stained jodhpurs, she wondered why she had thought he could ever be interested in her. He was going back to Hardwick Hall for a champagne reception, but she still had hours of work to do at the stables. They were worlds apart, she accepted with a heavy heart, and for her own good she had to stop mooning over him like a lovesick teenager.

Dusk was falling by the time she returned to her caravan, and she could summon little enthusiasm for the party which Earl Hardwick gave every year for guests and staff of the polo club. But she had promised Alex she would go, and so she stripped out of her filthy clothes and squeezed into the tiny shower cubicle.

'You look fantastic,' Alex greeted her when he arrived to drive her to the party. 'You should dress up more often, Rache.

I can't remember the last time I saw you in something other than jodhpurs.'

'I can hardly trip around the stables in a skirt and heels,' she pointed out. She felt ridiculously girly in her pink floral skirt and a silky chemise with delicate shoestring straps that left her shoulders bare. She had swept her hair up into a loose knot on top of her head, but it was so fine and silky that stray tendrils had already worked loose and framed her face. On an impulse, which she assured herself had nothing to do with the knowledge that Diego would be at the party, she was even wearing make-up—just a touch of mascara to darken her lashes and a pale pink gloss on her lips.

A huge marquee had been erected in the grounds of the Hardwick estate and the party was already in full swing when they arrived. Rachel's eyes were immediately drawn to Diego. Taller than everyone else in the room, his black tailored trousers and matching silk shirt emphasised his height and the breadth of his shoulders. With his dark hair falling onto his shoulders, and his gleaming olive skin, he was exotic and different, and other men paled into insignificance beside him.

She was not the only woman watching him, she noted moodily when she glanced around the marquee and saw that Felicity Hardwick and a gaggle of her aristocratic friends, all dressed in haute couture, were openly ogling him. Rachel instantly felt underdressed in her cheap skirt, which she'd bought from a market stall. Her arms ached from grooming fifteen polo ponies, and the evening suddenly seemed very flat. She was on her way over to the bar to tell Alex she was going home when Diego stepped into her path.

'Do you think your red-haired friend will object if I ask you to dance?' he murmured, his eyes gleaming with amusement and something else when Rachel's face flooded with colour.

'Alex and I are simply friends, and I'll dance with whoever I like,' she replied breathlessly, her heart racing as Diego caught her hand in his and slid his other arm around her waist.

'Then dance with me, *querida*,' he invited with a sultry smile that made her heart thud. 'You value your independence, don't you?' he commented, trying to focus on their conversation rather than the fire coursing through his veins when he drew Rachel's slender body against his thighs.

'More than anything,' she told him seriously. 'The most important lesson I learned from my mother's tangled love-life is that I don't want to be beholden to any man.'

She sounded so fierce that Diego's brows rose. 'Perhaps you have not yet found a man who excites you sufficiently that you would want to be beholden to him?'

'That's not likely to happen.' Rachel wondered what Diego would say if she admitted that *he* excited her unbearably. Since he had kissed her in her caravan they seemed to have been playing a waiting game where the sexual chemistry between them had simmered beneath the surface and they had both tried to ignore it. But the look in his eyes tonight told her that he was bored of the game. She could feel the tension in his body, and when he held her close so that her head rested on his chest she could hear the erratic beat of his heart and knew that it matched her own.

'What about marriage and children?' he queried curiously. 'Don't you want those?' Every woman he'd ever met had seemed to regard him as suitable husband material, and their first demand for commitment was invariably the point at which he ended a relationship. Rachel was a novelty in more ways than one, he brooded as he glanced down at her simple skirt and top and acknowledged that she looked sexier than any of the women at the party who were wearing designer outfits.

Rachel shrugged. 'I believe children deserve to have two parents who are committed to each other and, as I don't want to get married, I guess I won't have them. Perhaps I'll feel different in the future, but right now I don't have any maternal urges. I'd rather concentrate on my riding career.'

Diego's mouth curved into a smile that stole her breath. 'So, you are a free spirit and you can do whatever pleases you?'

'Yes.' The word escaped as a little gasp as he stroked his hand down to the base of her spine and exerted gentle pressure so that he brought her pelvis into direct contact with his. The hungry gleam in his eyes filled her with a feverish anticipation. Did he know how much he was pleasing her, holding her like this? How much she longed for him to lower his mouth to hers and kiss her as he had done two weeks ago?

He knew, she thought dreamily as their bodies swayed together in time with the music, one tune spilling into another so that she lost all sense of time and place and was conscious only of Diego—the hardness of his body and the subtle perfume of his aftershave, mingled with male pheromones that tantalised her senses. She didn't want to ever stop dancing, and felt a lurch of disappointment when the band announced they would be taking a break while the firework display took place. But, instead of releasing her, Diego kept his arm firmly around her waist as he led her outside and drew her to the edge of the crowd.

Starbursts of gold and silver shot across the sky and were reflected in the inky blackness of the lake. Rachel tilted her head to watch, supremely aware of Diego standing behind her, and she gave a little shiver when she felt him brush his lips down her neck in a feather-light caress.

The pyrotechnic display ended with a cascade of sparkling colours falling down to earth. There was a round of applause and, as the guests returned to the marquee, silence fell around them, a prickling, shimmering silence so intense that Rachel was aware of the faint, uneven whisper of her breath.

'It's not working, is it?' Diego murmured in her ear, his accent very pronounced and heart-stoppingly sexy.

Rachel turned to face him and shook her head, bemused by the question. 'What isn't?'

'Trying to ignore the hunger that is eating away at both of us,' he said softly.

She understood immediately, but understanding did not lessen her confusion. 'But you never gave any indication during the past two weeks that you wanted...' She broke off, her face flaming, and his smile widened into a predatory grin.

'You?' He finished her sentence for her. 'I promised myself that I would behave in a professional manner in the workplace. But that doesn't mean I have not secretly fantasised about barricading us in the hay barn and making love to you until we were both utterly sated.'

'Oh.' Rachel made a muffled sound, shocked not so much by his bluntness as the image in her head of him fulfilling his fantasy.

'Yes. *Oh*, Rachel.' Amusement lilted in his voice, but the expression in his eyes made her blood pound in her veins. 'The question is, *querida*—if we cannot ignore it, what are we going to do about it?'

His words hovered in the air between them, shredding her fragile composure. 'I don't know,' she whispered. But she did know, she acknowledged as every nerve-ending in her body tingled. He had aroused her sexual curiosity, and she wanted to explore the feelings he evoked in her, just as she wanted to explore the hard contours of his body and run her hands over his golden skin. There was no reason why she shouldn't go to bed with him. She was a single, independent woman who could live her life as she chose—but was he free?

'Are you involved with anyone at the moment?' she demanded baldly. She knew from what she'd read about him that Diego was seldom without female companionship!

'Definitely not.' Diego's eyes narrowed. 'Nor do I have any desire to be,' he told her firmly, needing to establish right away that he was not in the market for a relationship that demanded permanency or commitment. The past weeks had been purgatory as his desire for her had become a hungry monster that clamoured to be fed, and tonight, watching her dancing at the party in her floaty skirt which revealed her slender figure, he'd no longer been able to deny his fierce need. But, as with all his previous lovers—and there had been many, he owned unashamedly—a relationship with Rachel could only be on his terms.

'The party is almost over,' he said, flicking back the cuff of his dinner jacket and glancing at his Rolex. 'Do you want to come back with me—for coffee? Proper Argentinian coffee beans—' he tempted her with a smile '—not cheap powdered stuff.'

Rachel recalled his expression of disgust when he had sipped the coffee she had made him at her caravan. Diego was a millionaire and clearly never had to shop in discount supermarkets. It was a little thing, yet it emphasised the huge social divide between them. But, despite their different backgrounds, they were still just a man and a woman, and when passion had blazed between them two weeks ago the fact that she was a stable-girl and he was a wealthy world renowned polo player hadn't seemed to matter.

She could barely believe that he was asking her back—they both knew that the invitation was for more than coffee. With his stunning looks and blatant sex appeal he was spoilt for choice. He could have any woman he wanted. But the undisguised hunger in his eyes filled her with a fierce excitement that refused to listen to caution. Right now, Diego wanted her, and the knowledge made her tremble.

'All right,' she said shakily, but then paused as she remembered that he was staying at Hardwick Hall. 'I can't turn up at the Hall without an invitation from the Earl,' she murmured, wondering if Diego intended to smuggle her up to his room via the staff staircase.

'I am no longer the Hardwicks' house guest.' Diego ran his hands up her arms, savouring the feel of her satiny skin beneath his fingertips as he moved up to her shoulders and traced the fragile line of her collarbone. Every night since he had arrived in Gloucestershire, he had lain awake thinking about kissing her again, but now the waiting was over and he bent his head and brushed his mouth over hers, felt her tremble and wrapped his arms around her, aware that he couldn't kiss her as he wanted to yet.

'I like my own space, and I'm renting a cottage on the estate. It's situated in a very secluded part of the woods,' he added softly, grazing his lips over hers in a tantalising caress that promised so much more. 'I can guarantee we won't be disturbed all night.'

And if she left early in the morning, no one would know she had been there, Rachel realised, her excitement escalating once more now that her last nagging doubt had been dismissed. She would prefer not to be the subject of gossip and speculation among the estate staff.

'Well, then…' she murmured, her breath snagging in her throat when she glimpsed the predatory gleam in his eyes. Diego's mouth curved into a smile that made her pulse-rate accelerate. But, instead of kissing her again as she'd hoped, he caught hold of her hand and led her away from the marquee.

CHAPTER FOUR

DIEGO was staying in the old gamekeeper's cottage. The house was small and simply furnished, but Rachel barely noticed the décor when he ushered her inside and immediately pulled her into his arms. She couldn't quite believe she was here with Diego Ortega—internationally famous polo player and the man who had featured in the shockingly erotic fantasies she'd been having lately.

But her doubts were outweighed by a compelling certainty that this was somehow fated. She felt as though she had been waiting all her life for him, which was a dangerous thought, she acknowledged, because she was well aware that he would not be a part of her life for very long. She was under no illusions that Diego wanted anything more than sex with her—and perhaps he only wanted her for one night. But, far from being disappointed, she felt a sense of relief. She wasn't ready for a love affair; she valued her independence too much. Still, that didn't mean she had to live the life of a nun.

She found it difficult to think straight when he was sliding his fingertips lightly up and down her spine, and she could not restrain a little shiver when he brushed his lips along her collarbone and hovered over the pulse beating frenetically at the base of her throat.

'Would you like coffee, or a drink?' He eased away from her and took the two steps necessary to cross the tiny kitchen.

'There's champagne…or champagne,' he said, his sultry smile making her heart flip. He wasn't joking, Rachel realised when she glanced inside the fridge and saw that it was devoid of any basic necessities and instead contained two magnums of champagne and a jar of caviar.

He popped the cork with the same familiarity as most people would open a carton of milk, filled two glasses and handed her one of them. Rachel already felt dizzy—as if the bubbles fizzing in the glass had somehow entered her bloodstream, and when she sipped the pale gold liquid it seemed to be an elixir that swept away her doubts. She wished he would kiss her, and he must have read her mind because he put down his glass with a deliberation that set her heart thudding.

'Come here.'

His eyes gleamed gold beneath his heavy lids. Tiger's eyes, Rachel thought as she moved towards him. He was powerful and dominant and a part of her was appalled at how easily he could control her, but when he snaked his arm around her waist and jerked her up against him she could think of nothing but the hardness of his thighs pressed against hers, and the tantalising warmth of his body beneath his black silk shirt.

He took the clip from her hair and threaded his hands through the mass of gold silk that rippled down her back before claiming her mouth in a searing kiss that was shockingly demanding. 'You are so tiny,' he murmured when he finally lifted his lips from hers and straightened up so that he was once more towering over her. 'And so very lovely.' His gut clenched as he stared down at her delicate heart-shaped face. He couldn't remember ever feeling this overpowering need for a woman, this heavy drumbeat of desire that seemed to throb through his entire body. He had watched her and waited for her for two long weeks, and anticipation had added a certain piquancy to his desire, but now he could not wait a moment longer to possess her. 'We will definitely be more comfortable horizontal, *querida*,' he muttered hoarsely.

Horizontal meant bed, Rachel thought shakily, feeling a frisson of nervous excitement as the enormity of what she was about to do sank in. But he gave her no time for second thoughts. She gasped when he lifted her up, and she had no option but to wind her legs around his hips and curl her arms around his neck as he strode through the living room and up the narrow staircase to his bedroom. His hands cupped her bottom and, as he mounted the stairs, the feel of his hard arousal nudging between her thighs was so intensely erotic that heat flooded through her and she felt a heavy sensation deep in her pelvis.

'You see, much more comfortable,' he said thickly as he deposited her on the big bed and immediately stretched out next to her. Rachel had a vague impression of an airy white-walled room with dark wood ceiling beams and the bed with its carved headboard and crisp white cotton sheets. But then Diego leaned over her and the stark hunger she glimpsed in his eyes before he brought his mouth down on hers drove every thought from her mind except that she was lying on a bed with the man she had secretly idolised even before she had met him in the flesh.

His tongue probed between her lips until, with a gasp, she parted them and he thrust deep into her mouth in a sensual exploration. It was mind-blowing and she responded to him helplessly, sliding her fingers into his thick, silky hair as he trailed his lips down her throat and then lower to the faint swell of her breasts. Rachel held her breath, waiting for him to slide the straps of her top down her arms, but instead he slanted his mouth over one taut nipple straining against the silky material and sucked her wetly until she twisted her hips restlessly and felt a flooding warmth between her thighs.

He transferred his mouth to her other breast, and the feel of his tongue laving her through the now wet silk heightened her senses and her need to a level that was almost unbearable. But when he drew the straps of her top over her shoulders she could not prevent herself from tensing. No man had ever seen her naked before and she suddenly felt shy and unsure. Diego had dated some of the world's most beautiful women, super-models with stunning figures. But she was thin and her breasts were unexcitingly small, and she squeezed her eyes shut to block out the disappointment she was sure she would see in his as she felt him tug her top down to her waist.

'*Perfecto…*' he said raggedly. 'You are exquisite, *querida*.'

Startled by his husky tone, her eyes flew open and she swallowed at the expression in his dark gaze. 'You don't have to lie,' she mumbled, colour stealing into her cheeks when he cupped one pale mound in his hand. 'I hate being skinny and shapeless.'

'Not shapeless,' he insisted as he stroked her soft flesh and watched in fascination as her nipple hardened into a provocative peak that seemed to beg for him to take it into his mouth. 'You are as delicate and fragile as a porcelain figurine, and so fine boned that I'm afraid I will crush you beneath me.'

She trembled at the image in her head of him covering her body with his and bearing his weight down on her. Would he take it slowly? A bubble of hysteria rose in her throat as she imagined his response if she asked him to be gentle with her. She knew instinctively that if she revealed she was a virgin he would refuse to make love to her, and she could not bear for him to reject her. Before she had met Diego, she had believed she must have a low sex drive as none of the men she'd dated stirred her. Now she knew she had been waiting for the right man, but she needed to prove that she was not like her mother, and she would not confuse lust with love. She wanted to have sex with Diego, but that was all she wanted, and she was in complete control of her emotions, she assured herself.

'You won't crush me, I'm stronger than I look,' she told him softly, running her hands over his chest and fumbling with his shirt buttons, trying to disguise the fact that her fingers were shaking. She pushed the black silk aside and stroked his bare chest, loving the feel of his satiny skin overlaid with a covering of dark hairs. She had never touched a man before, and she studied his rippling abdominal muscles in fascination before sliding her hands up to explore his tight male nipples.

'I knew you would be a witch,' Diego said unsteadily. 'You have cast your spell over me. But now it is my turn to torment you, *mi belleza*.'

Rachel caught her breath when he lowered his head to her naked breast and painted moist circles around her nipple before taking the swollen peak fully into his mouth. Lost in the world of sensory pleasure he was creating, she lifted her hips so that he could remove her skirt, and she shivered when he slid his hand between her legs and stroked the sensitive flesh of her inner thigh. She could feel the sticky wetness between her legs and she was embarrassed by the unmistakable evidence that she was desperately aroused, especially when he hooked his fingers in the waistband of her tiny lace knickers and drew them slowly down.

'So lovely,' he said thickly as he ran his fingers over the triangle of gold curls he had exposed, before he gently parted her and eased between her slick velvet folds. 'And so very ready for me.' His voice was laced with rampant male satisfaction, but Rachel could not deny it and she arched her hips when he slid his finger deeper into her while his thumb pad found the ultra-sensitive nub of her clitoris and he caressed it until she sobbed his name.

'Please…' Everything was new and incredible and she wanted more, needed him to soothe the burning sensation in her pelvis.

'Soon, *querida*,' he promised as he suddenly sprang from the bed and tore off his shirt. 'I'm afraid this won't be a leisurely seduction. I want you now, and I can't wait—but you share my impatience, don't you, my Rachel?'

Her brain was barely capable of conscious thought, but as she dwelled on the phrase 'my Rachel' something tugged at her heart. It made her feel special, as if she was truly his, but no doubt he used the same endearment with all his lovers, she reminded herself, aware that it was important she took this for what it was—sex with no emotions involved on either side.

Diego dropped his shirt carelessly on the floor and as his hands moved to his belt Rachel stopped thinking and watched, wide-eyed, as he stripped off his trousers. His underwear could not disguise his fierce arousal, and her mouth ran dry when the boxers joined his trousers and she was faced with a naked and proudly erect male for the first time in her life.

Her immediate thought was that he wasn't going to fit—that sex between them was surely a physical impossibility. Up to this moment she had been driven by curiosity, and each new caress from his hands and mouth had increased her excitement. But now, as she stared at his rigid length, her doubts came storming back and she shrank back against the mattress when he came down beside her. Diego seemed unaware of her sudden tension, and when he brought his mouth down on hers and his long silky hair fell forwards to form a curtain around them both she forced herself to ignore her apprehension and kissed him back, running her hands over his muscular torso and feeling the hard ridges of his muscles.

'It has to be now, *querida*,' Diego muttered hoarsely. He hadn't been this turned on in years. He was so desperate for her he felt as though he was about to explode, and he swiftly positioned himself over her—and then stilled abruptly and cursed savagely in his native tongue.

Rachel could not understand the words, but the anger in his tone was unmistakable. She stared at him in bemusement. Had she done something wrong? she wondered fearfully. Could he have guessed that this was her first time?

'I'm sorry, Rachel. I did not expect to invite anyone back tonight and I don't have any protection,' he growled harshly, his frustration palpable.

Did she come under the label of 'anyone'? The unsettling

thought came into Rachel's head and brought home to her that Diego might just as easily have brought another woman from the party back to his cottage for casual sex. She pushed the thought away and concentrated on her relief that he was not rejecting her because he had somehow discovered that she was in unchartered territory.

'It's all right. I'm on the pill,' she murmured. After years of monthly misery her doctor had advised her to take it to regulate her periods, but she was aware that it was also the most reliable method of contraception.

The agonising frustration that had gripped Diego's body dissipated and excitement thundered through his veins. He was on fire for her and relieved that there was no reason why he could not make love to her. He refused to admit to the fleeting feeling of disappointment that her air of innocence which so intrigued him was not real, and that she was obviously sexually experienced.

Instead, he slid his hands beneath her bottom and angled her for his possession. His penis strained urgently against her moist opening and he slowly eased forwards, a shudder running through him as her tight muscles closed around him and clasped him in a velvet embrace. As he entered her, his eyes locked with hers and he was puzzled by her expression—the look of wonderment and surprise, as if this was all new to her. She was so incredibly tight… He frowned as he withdrew a little and then thrust deeper into her, heard her faint gasp. 'Rachel…?'

'It's been a while,' she mumbled shyly.

He stared down at her pink cheeks and saw that she was embarrassed, and he felt an unexpected surge of tenderness mixed with arrogant male satisfaction that she had obviously not had a lover for months—or maybe even longer.

'Then we'll take it slowly,' he assured her. But, as he sank deeper inside her and established a sensual rhythm that matched the pounding beat of his heart, his resolve was tested to its limits. She was the most responsive lover he had ever known, he could already feel his pleasure building and knew that he would not be able to hold back for long.

The slight discomfort she had felt when Diego had first thrust into her was less than Rachel had expected and soon forgotten as he slowly filled her. It was good; better than good—awesome, amazing, she thought shakily as she curved her legs around his hips and drew him deeper into her. She caught her breath when he withdrew almost completely and then drove into her again and again, faster now as his pace became more urgent.

She could not think, could only feel, every cell in her body attuned to the intense sensations he was arousing in her. She had not expected the act of lovemaking to be so beautiful; to feel that not just her body but her soul was joined with Diego, and for some inexplicable reason tears stung her eyes. She blinked them away frantically and pressed her face into the tanned column of his throat, brushing her mouth over the pulse that jerked beneath his skin.

She never wanted him to stop, and yet there had to be an end—he could not keep up this frenetic rhythm for ever. The throbbing ache low in her pelvis was growing ever more insistent. And then suddenly she was hovering on the brink of the unknown, and she was almost afraid of what would come next as Diego thrust deeper and harder than before and she felt herself explode in a shattering wave of ecstasy. Spasm after spasm of pleasure ripped through her, so intense that she cried out and clung to his sweat-slicked shoulders while he slammed into her and then gave a harsh groan, his big body shuddering and his head thrown back as he reached his own spectacular climax.

For a few moments afterwards they remained joined, and Rachel revelled in the weight and warmth of his body pressing down on her. She could stay like this for ever, she thought dreamily as she slid her fingers through his hair and stroked her hands across his massive shoulders. She felt safe and protected in the arms of this big, powerful man—and after her childhood, where she had received little care or affection, the feeling that she somehow belonged with Diego was sweetly seductive. But it was also dangerous, she conceded when he finally rolled off her and tucked his arms behind his head. For a few seconds she felt bereft and longed to cuddle up to him, but instinct warned her that he would be horrified if she clung to him.

Instead, she affected a tiny yawn, even though she had never felt more awake in her life, and allowed her lashes to drift down so that she could stare at him without him being aware of her compulsion to study every minute detail of his face until it was imprinted on her memory for ever.

Diego turned his head and glanced at Rachel. Her long eyelashes fanned her cheeks and her lips were slightly parted, reddened and swollen from the demanding pressure of his mouth. With her golden hair spilling over the pillow, she looked young and ridiculously innocent, and he felt a curious tugging sensation in his chest. He had known that sex with her would be good, and it had exceeded all his expectations, but he had not expected the experience to be so…shattering—a complete union of body and mind that had left him feeling more content than he could ever remember.

'You haven't done this much before, have you?' he murmured.

Her lashes flew upwards and cornflower-blue eyes regarded him warily. 'What do you mean?' Had he realised that it had been her first time? If so, he did not appear to be annoyed, Rachel decided, her flutter of panic fading.

'I mean, I do not think you have had many lovers,' Diego said carefully. He did not understand why he was probing for information about her exes. Never before had he been curious about a woman's past history, and it shouldn't matter to him if Rachel had had dozens of other men, he brooded irritably.

Rachel was silent for so long that he thought she was not

going to answer. 'Not many, no,' she admitted quietly, blushing profusely. 'I'm sorry if I disappointed you.'

Diego refused to question why he was so inordinately pleased with her reply. 'You were incredible, *querida*,' he assured her in a deep growl that made the tiny hairs on her body stand on end. 'Does this feel as if I was disappointed?' he murmured as he took her hand and placed it on his hardening manhood.

Rachel caught her breath when she felt him swell beneath her fingertips until his erection was a rigid shaft of muscle. 'Do you want to do it again?' she asked him in a startled voice. Her heartbeat was only just returning to normal, but the idea that he wanted her again, so soon after the first time, sent her pulse-rate soaring.

She must know the effect that her breathlessly innocent query had on him, Diego brooded as savage hunger surged through him. It was a clever trick designed to make a man feel as though he was her first lover, but the knowledge that she was an adept game player did not lessen his desire, and he gave a self-derisive laugh as he slid his hand between her legs and discovered her slick wetness.

'What do you think?' he said harshly and, without giving her time to reply, he moved over her and entered her with one hard, powerful thrust, smothering her soft gasp with his mouth as he began the whole delicious process of making love to her all over again.

Rachel was used to waking early, and when she opened her eyes the bedroom was shadowed with the pearly grey light that preceded dawn. She stretched, and winced as the effects of the previous night on her untutored body made themselves known. Diego was still asleep; she could hear the rhythmic sound of his breathing and she turned her head and studied him, absorbing the masculine beauty of his sculpted features and the faint dark stubble on his chin with a faint sense of desperation that she would probably never lie like this with him again.

She had no experience of how to behave after a one-night stand. Should she wait for him to wake up, and maybe they would share a leisurely breakfast? Recalling the sparse contents of his fridge, breakfast seemed unlikely. And she could not picture herself making small talk with him when memories of the incredible and sometimes shocking things he had done to her last night were making her blush.

She needed some time alone to come to terms with the fact that she had given her virginity to a man who was practically a stranger. She knew very little about him, other than that he owned a ranch just outside Buenos Aires. He never spoke of his family or his private life and although sex with him last night had been incredible, and she definitely did not regret it, she was no nearer to understanding what made Diego Ortega tick.

It seemed sensible to slip away now, before he or the rest of the estate were awake, but she was reluctant to move. Diego was lying on his back with one arm flung across her stomach—although, when he had finally allowed her to fall asleep, he had rolled away from her onto his side of the bed. Some time during the night their bodies had drawn closer together and she felt loath to break the connection between them.

But the feeling of closeness was a dangerous illusion, she told herself firmly as she eased carefully from beneath the sheet. The morning air was cool and she shivered as she donned her skirt and flimsy top. At this hour she would normally be wearing jodhpurs and a thick sweatshirt, and she prayed none of the estate workers would be about to comment on her appearance.

'What are you doing, *querida*? Do you know what the time is?' The seductive drawl—husky from sleep—sent a frisson of fierce awareness down her spine.

Diego propped himself up on one elbow and surveyed Rachel indolently. It had been an amazing night. He had known instinctively that sex between them would be mind-blowing, and he hadn't been wrong. His body had been utterly sated when he'd finally fallen asleep, but the sight of her in the pale light of dawn, flushed and still sleepy, with her golden hair rippling down her back, caused a familiar tightening in his groin and he acknowledged that one night of her was not going to be nearly enough.

'Why are you up so early?' he murmured.

'I'm a stable-hand—one of the requisites of my job is to get up early.'

His eyes narrowed as he caught the faint defensive note in her voice. 'Not on a Sunday,' he said lazily. He patted the sheet. 'Come back to bed.'

'Horses have to be fed and turned out, even on a Sunday.' Rachel ignored the fact that this was her Sunday off and fought her longing to do as Diego had said and get back into bed with him. The sultry gleam in his eyes told her that he was not inviting her to go back to sleep, and her body was clamouring to experience his soul-shattering brand of magic one more time. 'I need to go,' she muttered, forcing herself to walk over to the door.

'It's 5:00 a.m.' Diego could not hide his frustration when it became apparent that Rachel was actually going to leave. Women did not usually walk out on him after a night in his bed. In fact, this was the first time ever, and another first was his brief flare of self-doubt that he had not satisfied her last night. He dismissed it instantly as he recalled how she had writhed beneath him. No way had she been faking it. He had given her orgasm after orgasm, and the moans and cries she had emitted as she'd tossed her head from side to side on the pillow had been ample proof that he had pleased her.

'If I wait any longer people might see me leaving the cottage,' she mumbled.

'What *people*?'

'People who work on the estate—groundsmen, the other grooms—my colleagues!' Rachel said tersely, flushing when Diego stared at her as if she had taken leave of her senses. 'I don't want anyone to know I spent the night here.'

Diego shook his head, mystified by Rachel's change of mood from the sensual sex kitten of last night to someone who was decidedly on edge this morning. 'Why not?'

'Because word will get round that we had a one-night stand,' she told him impatiently. 'I'd prefer not to have my private life open to public discussion, and I assumed you would feel the same way.'

'I don't give a damn what anyone else thinks,' Diego stated with such supreme arrogance that Rachel's temper simmered. 'And what makes you think that either of us would be content with only one night together? We were dynamite between the sheets and I want you in my bed every night.'

Every night while he was staying at Hardwick, Rachel quickly reminded herself as her heart leapt. She could not suppress her excitement that he seemed to want an affair with her, but it was vital to remember that their relationship would only be temporary.

'I don't object to seeing you again,' she said carefully, 'but I don't want anyone else to know about us. In a few weeks you'll go back to Argentina, but I'll still work here after you've gone and I hate the idea of being the subject of gossip.'

'So you don't object to seeing me again?' he repeated in a dangerously soft tone. Dark brows winged upwards in an expression of haughty disdain. 'How very magnanimous of you, *querida*,' Diego snapped, outraged that Rachel seemed to think she could call the shots in their relationship. 'But how exactly are we to meet up in secret? Do you intend for us to creep through the estate after dark like criminals? If you are ashamed of being with me, then I can see little point in continuing with this,' he stated coldly.

Rachel's stomach dipped at the finality in his voice, but at the same time her temper flared. 'I'm not ashamed of being with you, but I think you should try seeing it from my point of view,' she muttered. 'I don't want to be for ever known locally as the woman who once had a brief fling with the notorious playboy Diego Ortega. I do have some pride, you know.'

'Then I suggest you take your pride and get out,' Diego growled furiously, struggling to contain his outrage at the notion of engaging in some cloak-and-dagger affair with Rachel. In his past, every woman he had ever dated had been eager to broadcast their affair with him, and he had always hated the publicity. But, far from being pleased that Rachel wanted to keep her relationship with him a secret, he was deeply insulted. He glared at her, waiting for her to back down, but her mouth was set in a mutinous line and she glared right back at him.

'Fine,' she said crisply as she yanked open the door. 'Well, it was nice knowing you…' She broke off abruptly, and Diego felt a spurt of satisfaction when her face burned with fiery colour.

'Ditto,' he drawled sardonically, still not quite able to believe that she would walk out of the door. 'Just remember when you are tossing and turning in your lonely bed tonight that you can thank your pride for the sexual frustration which prevents you from sleeping.'

His arrogance was unbelievable! Rachel made a strangled sound as she marched out onto the landing and she vented her temper by slamming the door after her and then kicked it for good measure, incensed by the sound of Diego's mocking laughter following her down the stairs.

CHAPTER FIVE

RACHEL might have guessed that a day that had started off so badly would get progressively worse. Keeping to the woodland paths, she saw no one on her journey back to her caravan, but once there she was too worked up to relax—her anger with Diego mixed with a growing feeling that once again she had handled things badly. Far from regarding her as a one night stand, Diego had made it clear that he had hoped to have an affair with her, at least for the duration of his stay at Hardwick—and she had thrown his invitation straight back in his face.

She was thankful when one of the other grooms phoned her, pleading a hangover from last night's party and begging her to work his shift at the stables. At least being busy would stop her from dwelling on things she'd rather not think about, she brooded as she cycled into the yard. Things like her wanton response when Diego had made love to her, and the fact that, thanks to her stubborn streak and hot temper, he now wanted nothing more to do with her.

The cool dawn gave way to another unusually warm day for May, and by mid-morning Rachel felt hot and tired after a serious lack of sleep the previous night. Usually she always took extra care around Earl Hardwick's bad tempered mare, Poppy, but for once she was careless and forgot to muzzle the horse before starting to groom her. Poppy was at her most uncooperative, shaking her head wildly before snapping her teeth into an expanse of bared flesh—eliciting a startled cry of pain from Rachel as she stared at the bite mark on her upper arm.

The bite had broken her skin and when she met Alex later in the afternoon the bandage she'd tied around the wound was soaked with blood. Alex took one look at it and ignoring her protests, bundled her into his car and drove her to the accident and emergency unit of the local hospital.

'You can't take chances, Rache,' he told her when she emerged two hours later with her arm swathed in a sterile dressing and clutching a week's course of antibiotics. 'Animal bites are prone to infection.'

The doctor who had dressed her wound had said the same thing, and as soon as Rachel got home she followed his advice and took a double dose of the antibiotic before she set about scrubbing the interior of the caravan in an effort to expend some of her restless energy. She would not waste another second thinking about Diego, she told herself when she dumped the now curled and brown roses he had given her two weeks ago in the bin. She was kneeling in front of her tiny fridge, debating whether the cheese would be safe to eat if she scraped the mould off it, when the sound of a familiar, toe-curlingly sexy voice made her jump to her feet.

'You can't possibly be contemplating eating that, not unless you want another trip to the hospital with food poisoning.' Diego walked up the steps of the caravan and filled the doorway, looking so gorgeous in faded denims and a white T-shirt which contrasted with his bronzed skin that Rachel's heart seemed to temporarily stop beating. 'How's the arm?'

'Fine,' she replied automatically, despite the fact that her wound was throbbing painfully. She frowned. 'How did you know…?'

He shrugged. 'Word travels fast on the estate.'

'Exactly my point,' Rachel muttered tersely. 'If anyone had seen me coming out of your cottage this morning in the clothes I'd been wearing the night before, gossip would have swept through the estate faster than wildfire.'

'I realise that now.' His quietly spoken comment was so surprising after their earlier row that Rachel stared at him, wishing she could see his expression, which was hidden behind his designer shades. 'Everyone at Hardwick seems to know everyone else's business,' Diego said, sounding faintly irritated. It was his first experience of life in a close-knit rural community and he was amazed by the fascination that everyone, from Earl Hardwick down to the assistant gardener, took in their neighbours' day-to-day affairs.

He had spent most of the day in a furious temper after Rachel had walked out on him, but by late afternoon his anger had faded as he acknowledged she had every right to want to protect her privacy. Last night had been amazing, and he'd come to the conclusion that the passion they had shared had been too electrifying to throw away.

He glanced at her, noting the wariness in her eyes, and wondered if she had any idea how badly he wanted her. What was it about this delicate English girl with her pale-as-milk skin and a dusting of gold freckles on her nose that he found such a turn on? he brooded irritably. Her close-fitting jodhpurs emphasised her boyishly slim hips and her tight, faded T-shirt looked fit for the rag bag. But, despite her lack of sophistication, he ached to release the clip that secured her hair in an untidy knot on top of her head and run his fingers through the heavy silk, and he was already envisaging pushing her shirt up so that he could cradle her firm breasts in his hands.

'I was wondering if you'd like to join me for dinner. At the cottage, naturally, as we dare not risk being seen dining together in public at the Rose and Crown,' he added dryly.

Rachel went pink but ignored his jibe, her pulse quickening at the realisation that he seemed to be giving her another chance. 'Do you mean you're going to cook?' she queried, recalling the lonely jar of caviar in his fridge and trying to imagine him pushing a trolley around the local supermarket.

'*Santa Madre*. No!' He sounded as shocked as if she had suggested flying to Mars. He removed his sunglasses and shook his glossy dark hair back from his face. 'I've discovered an excellent French restaurant in Harrowbridge—and, even better, I've persuaded the manager to start up a home delivery service,' he explained, his eyes glinting with amusement when he noted the conflicting emotions on Rachel's face. 'Of course, you may not like French food, *querida*, in which case I will try my powers of persuasion on the Italian eatery at the other end of the town.'

'French will be lovely,' Rachel murmured after a long pause, ignoring the fact that she had never actually eaten French food. Dinner wasn't the real issue here, and they both knew it.

'I've left my car down by the farmhouse. Come with me now and I'll drop you back here early in the morning—before anyone's about,' Diego suggested casually.

His smile was a lethal weapon that numbed her brain and turned her legs to jelly, and she began to appreciate the very real danger he presented to her peace of mind. In the five years that she had worked as a groom at Hardwick she had fought to prove she was 'one of the lads' in an industry that was still rife with male chauvinism. But, for the first time in her life, she was tempted to sacrifice the respect she had earned among the other grooms and brazenly advertise the fact that she had slept with Diego to anyone who cared to know.

Nothing seemed to matter other than knowing he wanted her in his bed, and a little part of her longed for him to sweep her into his arms and kiss her senseless before carrying her to his car and driving her through the estate to his cottage, uncaring of the curiosity and speculation they would arouse. Although he was staring at her intently, he made no attempt to persuade her and the voice of caution in her head grew louder, reminding her of the lessons she'd learned after witnessing her parents' tangled love lives—no one was worth losing her independence for.

'I need to shower and sort out a few things, and then I'll cycle over to the cottage,' she told him in a cool voice that disguised her feverish excitement at the thought of spending another night with him. 'That way, I can ride my bike home again tomorrow.'

Diego's eyes narrowed, but he controlled his spurt of irritation. Everything with Rachel was a battle of wills, but that made his ultimate victory all the sweeter, he reminded himself. And it was satisfying to know that soon she would not be arguing with him, but pleading for his possession as she had done the previous night. 'Suit yourself,' he murmured with a faint shrug. 'But instead of a shower, why not have a bath at the cottage? I've always found that a long, hot soak is the best way to relax tired muscles.'

The wicked gleam in his eyes brought a rush of colour to Rachel's cheeks as she acknowledged that the reason why she ached all over was because of the demands he had made on her body last night. But the idea of sinking into the enormous roll-top bath at the cottage was irresistible. 'That sounds good,' she murmured. The sexual tension that had been smouldering between them since he had arrived was suddenly so acute that her skin prickled, and anticipation caused a dragging ache low in her pelvis.

He nodded and walked down the caravan steps, but halted at the bottom and turned back to her. His face was on level with hers and he dropped a brief, stinging kiss on her mouth that left her aching for more. 'Don't keep me waiting too long, *querida*,' he drawled. 'I'm ravenous!'

The predatory glint in Diego's eyes stayed with Rachel long after he strode down the track back to his car. Not knowing what she would need, she simply grabbed clean clothes for tomorrow and her toothbrush and bundled them into a backpack. Twenty minutes later she was cycling through the woods, retracing the path she had walked earlier that morning, back to the cottage.

She found the front door ajar, but when she walked into the hall there was no sign of Diego. From above came the sound of running water and she hurried up the stairs, coming to an abrupt halt when she pushed open the bathroom door and discovered him immersed in a bath full of foaming bubbles, sipping champagne.

'Hello, beautiful,' he drawled, raising his glass and greeting her with a smile that stole her breath.

'Didn't you say dinner is going to be delivered?' she croaked, her eyes locked on his muscular chest and the whorls of damp black hairs visible between the bubbles. He was so impossibly gorgeous. She felt weak with wanting him, but her instinct for self-protection warned her that it was imperative she did not allow herself to be swept away by his sexy charm.

'It'll be here in a couple of hours.'

Her heart began to thud unevenly as she speculated on how he intended to fill the time until dinner arrived. 'I thought you were hungry.'

'Join me in this bath and I'll show you just how hungry I am, *querida*,' he promised her deeply, the amusement in his eyes changing to an expression of such feral need that Rachel trembled. Last night this had all been new to her, but tonight she knew what to expect and she was overwhelmed by an urgent need to feel him inside her. She gripped the hem of her T-shirt—but then paused. Evening sunlight was streaming through the bathroom window and she felt reluctant to strip in front of him. It would be fine if she possessed voluptuous curves and was slipping out of a sexy negligee, but she was thin and bony and wearing jodhpurs and one of her oldest T-shirts.

'Diego…' She opened her mouth to tell him that she would undress in the bedroom, but he interrupted her.

'Take it off.' His voice was slurred and heavy with desire,

causing molten heat to flood through her veins. Slowly she lifted her arms, tugged her shirt over her head and dropped it on the floor, blushing when his eyes focused intently on her breasts.

'Now the rest.'

There was no elegant way to kick off her riding boots and shimmy out of her jodhpurs, but Diego discovered that watching Rachel removing her clothes was the most erotic striptease he had ever witnessed. He was thankful that the bubbles hid the solid length of his arousal when he stared at her naked, slender body with her spun-gold hair spilling over her shoulders to cover her breasts, and the cluster of blonde curls between her legs.

'You are the most beautiful woman I've ever known,' he said harshly. The words were torn from him—he was shaken by his reaction to her. He was an expert in giving glib compliments to his lovers, but Rachel's pale loveliness evoked a curious ache inside him that he refused to assimilate. Instead he set down his champagne glass and held out his hand to assist her as she stepped gracefully into the bath.

'I need to keep the dressing on my arm dry,' she murmured when he drew her down into the foaming water. 'Diego—what is that…?' She broke off, her face flaming as he settled her on his thighs and she felt his rigid shaft push into her belly.

He laughed at her shocked expression and felt his heart-rate quicken as her shock turned to undisguised excitement when he slid his hand between her legs. 'Rest your arm on the side of the bath,' he bade her in a low growl, 'and allow me the pleasure of washing you.'

'Diego…' Rachel drew a sharp breath when he picked up a bar of soap and smoothed it over her breasts, washing her with a thoroughness that made her tremble. He rinsed her just as assiduously, first with his hands and then, when he had rolled her nipples between his fingers until they swelled and hardened, he lowered his head and took one and then the other into his mouth, sucking deeply until she gave a guttural moan and gripped his hair, desperate for him to stop and equally desperate for him to continue his sorcery.

He had positioned her so that she was lying back in the bath and he was kneeling over her, the dark curtain of his hair falling forwards to brush against her skin as he at last took mercy on her and lifted his mouth from her breast to her lips. And, while he kissed her, he slid the soap over her stomach and then lower, stroking and exploring her in an erotic foreplay that went beyond the wildest excesses of Rachel's imagination.

'I really think I'm clean,' she gasped as she twisted frantically, sending bath water slopping onto the floor.

'Then I'd better help to dry you,' Diego murmured as he stepped out of the bath, roughly dried himself and then scooped her out of the water and enfolded her in a towel. He carried her through to the bedroom and blotted the moisture from her body with the same dedication that he had washed her, until she was sure she would die with wanting him. She was on fire for him and ran her hands eagerly over his chest, trying to urge him down, but he laughed softly and drew her arms down by her sides.

'You should always moisturise your skin after a bath,' he told her, his amber eyes gleaming with a wicked intent that made her heart pound as he took a bottle of lotion from the bedside table and tipped fragrant oil into his palms.

This was a well-planned seduction—a routine he'd probably performed on numerous occasions with his previous lovers, cautioned a quiet voice of common sense in Rachel's head. But it didn't matter; nothing seemed to matter except that he should ease the ache of sexual frustration that was tearing at her insides.

He started at her feet, massaging the scented oil into her skin with sensuous strokes, and by the time he reached her breasts and brushed his fingertips back and forth across her nipples she sobbed his name and begged him to take her—now, this minute. He gave a husky laugh at her eagerness as he dipped slick, oiled fingers between her thighs, gently parted her and discovered the flooding sweetness of her arousal and, to Rachel's feverish relief, he finally positioned himself over her.

'Are you ready, *querida*?'

Was she? If she was any more turned on she would melt. 'Diego…*please*…' Last night she'd suffered a few last-minute doubts when he had rubbed the solid length of his erection up and down the outer lips of her vagina, but tonight she was frantic for him to fill her. She opened her legs, bending her knees a little and catching her breath when he entered her with one deep, powerful thrust which felt so incredibly good that she sighed her pleasure against his mouth.

He made love to her with all his considerable skill, exerting superb control and taking her to the edge once, twice, until she writhed beneath him, wantonly begging him to take her harder, faster, and crying out when he relented and thrust so deep that she climaxed in a violent explosion of ecstasy. Only then did he relinquish his grip on his self-control and he reached the heights seconds after her, giving a low groan as he pumped his seed into her.

In the aftermath Rachel felt limp and spent as her heart-rate gradually slowed. Diego was an incredible lover, she mused. She had no one to compare him with, but she knew instinctively that sex would never get any better than this. But there was no point in hoping that they would ever share anything more than passion. In a few weeks he would return to Argentina and it was likely that she would never see him again—and that suited her fine, she reminded herself, trying to ignore the way her heart leapt when he rolled off her and immediately curled his arm around her and drew her against his chest. She had her life mapped out—her riding ambitions were paramount but there was no reason why she should not enjoy a brief love affair with Diego, safe in the knowledge that neither of them wanted anything more than fantastic sex.

CHAPTER SIX

'CHECKMATE.' Diego moved his bishop and then leaned back on his elbow and grinned at Rachel.

'What…?' She stared down at the travel-sized chessboard set out on the picnic rug and shook her head in dismay. 'But I was about to win. I had my strategy all planned out.'

'But instead I win again. You know what this means, *querida*?' Diego's eyes glinted wickedly. 'The loser forfeits an item of clothing—and, as you have already lost your shoes and bracelet, this time it has to be your dress.'

'You can't really expect me to take it off here,' Rachel argued, feeling her heart begin to thud hard beneath her ribs. 'We're in a public place…and I'm not wearing a bra.'

'I know.' The look of devilment in Diego's gaze was mixed with a sensual gleam that sent a quiver of excitement down Rachel's spine. 'I have been painfully aware all day that the only thing hiding your breasts from my eyes is a very thin cotton dress. But you can't hide from me any longer. We're miles from the nearest village, and we've picnicked at this spot three times before and never seen a soul—so come on, hand it over.'

Rachel knew she was beaten. 'I can't believe you talked me into playing strip chess in the first place,' she grumbled, 'especially when I've only just learned the game.' She began to tug at the buttons that ran down the front of her dress, flushing beneath Diego's avid stare. Two could play at teasing, she decided—and, when she had unfastened the dress to her waist, she slowly drew it down to expose her shoulders and breasts, feeling a spurt of feminine triumph when dull colour flared along Diego's cheekbones.

'I bet it isn't one of the rules that the loser has to undress,' she said as she allowed the dress to slither down her thighs until it pooled at her feet and she stood before him wearing only a pair of minuscule lace panties.

They had spread the picnic rug beneath an oak tree, and the sun filtering through the leaves dappled Rachel's slender body. She looked like a woodland nymph, Diego brooded, feeling his body harden.

'It's in the Argentinian rule book,' he assured her gravely, his lips twitching. His eyes settled on the fragile wisp of lace between her thighs, and he gave her a predatory smile. 'Want to play again? Loser loses…everything.'

Rachel gave a little gasp as he suddenly tugged her ankle so that she tumbled down on top of him, and her pulse raced as he placed his hands on her bottom and clamped her tightly against him so that she could feel his arousal straining beneath his jeans. 'You might lose, and then you would have to strip,' she pointed out, her eyes dancing with amusement that swiftly darkened to desire when he grazed his lips along her collarbone.

'That's the plan, *cariño*,' he said throatily.

Rachel's laughter echoed around the sunny copse, but the sound was soon lost beneath the pressure of Diego's mouth on hers. Life was a lot like chess—complicated and unpredictable—she mused as she anchored her fingers in his long silky hair. She had never had an affair before, and so hadn't known what to expect, certainly not that she and Diego would become friends, as well as lovers, over the last few weeks. They shared everything and spent all their time together, although at the stables they tried to keep their relationship a secret from the other grooms.

Every night their passion grew more intense, but the bond that Rachel felt with Diego was based not just on sex, but on laughter and long conversations about every subject under the sun. On evenings and weekends they saddled up the horses and rode out together, exploring the beauty of the Cotswolds beneath cloudless blue skies.

Falling in love with him was not in the rule book, but day by day her emotions were becoming more entangled. The summer was racing past, and in a few more weeks he was due to return to Argentina. But he wasn't going yet, she consoled herself, and a lot could happen in a few weeks. They might fall out and be glad to see the back of each other—or he might fall for her…

While she had been daydreaming he had shrugged out of his clothes and she smiled at him as he moved over her, and felt the familiar tug on her heart when he smiled back. Who could tell what the future held?

Diego propped himself up on one elbow and stared at Rachel curled up beside him. Her lips were slightly parted and the sunlight filtering through the gap in the curtains turned her hair to a river of gold on the pillows. It was a month since they had become lovers, and he was faintly surprised that his fascination with her was even stronger than when he had first taken her to bed.

He could lie here watching her for hours, he mused, frowning slightly as he realised how quickly he had grown used to her sharing his bed—and his life. Usually she woke first—to the strident ring of her alarm clock, which was set for some ungodly hour before dawn—and normally she was dressed and about to sneak back to her caravan when he stirred. But last night he had switched off the alarm, and obviously making love to her three times during the night had worn her out because she was still fast asleep.

She would need food, he decided, swinging his legs over

the side of the bed and carefully tucking the sheet around her. She would need to replenish the energy she'd used last night and, although he could not face anything more than strong black coffee in the mornings, Rachel was a breakfast girl.

Pulling on his robe, he padded barefoot down to the kitchen and found a saucepan, milk and the porridge oats Rachel ate every morning. He had watched her make her breakfast a dozen times, but he still managed to burn the milk, and he cursed as he stared at the lumpy grey goo he'd ended up with. A vigorous stir seemed to help and he added syrup, poured juice into a glass and, on an impulse he refused to question, he stepped outside and snipped off a pink rosebud, which he placed on the tray before he returned to the bedroom.

She was still asleep and looked so peaceful that he was reluctant to disturb her. He couldn't get enough of her, he acknowledged silently—and it was not just because she was a wild temptress in bed. She was good company and he liked having her around. He liked her sharp wit and her wicked sense of humour, and her infectious giggle that never failed to make him smile. He was even considering taking her to New York with him. He would only be at Hardwick for one more week and then planned to spend a month at his polo school in the States, before returning to Argentina. He was confident he would have tired of Rachel before he went home, and he certainly had no intention of inviting her to the Estancia Elvira. However, he was not convinced she would fit in with his lifestyle in New York—and, if he was honest, he'd arranged their forthcoming trip to London as a test to see how she coped in social situations.

Rachel stretched lazily beneath the sheets and slowly became conscious of soft golden sunlight stealing beneath her eyelids. Sunlight! Her lashes flew open and for a second she studied the chiselled perfection of Diego's face, his jaw shaded with dark stubble that seemed to enhance his sexiness. But then she grabbed her alarm clock and gave a horrified yelp.

'It's nearly nine o'clock!' She'd never slept that late in her life. 'My alarm can't have gone off.'

'It would seem so.' His amused drawl sparked her temper and she glared at him, pushing her tangled hair out of her eyes impatiently.

'I'm late for work. Why didn't you wake me?'

'Because you're not going to work for the next couple of days,' he said cheerfully. 'Here, I've made your breakfast.' He set the tray down on Rachel's lap and she stared at the brimming bowl of porridge in disbelief.

'*You* made it?' she said faintly. Diego was a sex-god and a world class polo player, but he was utterly clueless in the kitchen. She picked up the rosebud and gave him a smile that stole his breath. 'Thank you.'

'You'd better save your thanks until after you've tried it,' he said gruffly, dragging his eyes from the tempting curve of her breasts, barely concealed beneath the sheet.

'I'm sure it's lovely.' She would eat it even if it was foul because he had made it for her and, despite the lumps, she forced the porridge down, drank the juice and then remembered what he had said. 'What did you mean about me not going to work? Of course I'm going.'

'Uh-uh.' He put the tray on the dresser, slid out of his robe and joined her in the bed, tugging her down on top of him and clamping her hips when she wriggled to escape him. The frantic squirming of her hips intensified his arousal—and hers, he noted, watching the way her eyes darkened with desire.

'Diego…?' Rachel gasped and fought to retain her sanity.

'I have to attend a business meeting in London, and I thought you would like to come with me.'

'To your meeting?' She frowned in confusion.

'To shop—in preparation for our trip to Royal Ascot.' He grinned at her stunned expression. 'A friend of mine has hired a private box for Ladies' Day and invited me to bring a guest. I want you to be my guest, *querida*.'

'I've always wanted to go to Ascot,' Rachel admitted slowly, excitement at the idea of visiting the famous horse-racing event drowning out the voice in her head which pointed out that Diego had altered the rules of their relationship without asking her.

For the past month they had maintained the act of a professional working relationship in front of the other staff at Hardwick. Now he was suggesting being seen together in public—but it was unlikely that they would bump into anyone she knew at Ascot, she reassured herself. She stared down at him, feeling her heart give its familiar flip as she absorbed the male beauty of his face, and accepted that she was desperate to go with him.

'I don't need to go shopping,' she told him firmly. Ascot would be heaven, but trekking around the shops was her idea of hell. 'I bought a new outfit for a friend's wedding last summer and I'm sure it will do.'

'And I'm equally sure it won't,' he murmured dryly. 'You can't walk into the Royal Enclosure in a cheap, off-the-peg dress. While I'm at my meeting I've arranged for a personal stylist to take you to Bond Street and find you something suitable to wear.

'Humour me, *querida*?' he said softly when she opened her mouth to protest, and he took advantage of her parted lips to slide his tongue between them at the same time as he lifted her and guided her down onto his swollen length, smiling triumphantly when he heard her gasp as he filled her. It was the most effective way he knew of stalling the argument he could sense was brewing. Rachel was feisty and independent—but she was totally addicted to him and he had no compunction about using sex to get his own way.

They drove to London later that morning. Rachel wanted to go back to the caravan and pick up clothes and toiletries, and had hoped to dash up to the stables and see Piran, but Diego's meeting was scheduled for early afternoon and he was impatient to get away.

'You can buy everything you need in town,' he told her as they sped along the motorway, 'and I've arranged for one of the other grooms to exercise Piran for the next few days.'

She felt as though her independence was being subtly eroded, Rachel fretted silently. A month ago she wouldn't have dreamed of allowing anyone else to take charge of Piran, and she was disturbed that Diego had organised the trip—and her life, it seemed—without consulting her.

During her childhood she had lived through her mother's various love affairs—which had usually resulted in the upheaval of moving into a new home and being expected to get on with new step-siblings. Liz Summers had put everything into her relationships and sacrificed her independence without a second thought—only to be devastated when it all went wrong a few months down the line. Rachel had vowed that she would never allow a man to take over her life, but nothing had prepared her for Diego's charismatic personality—or her overwhelming need for him. For the first time she appreciated the power of sexual attraction. It would be very easy to be swept away by him, she acknowledged—she was already halfway there.

She had assumed that they would stay in a hotel in London, and she gave Diego a puzzled glance when he parked in a private car park close to the river. 'Who lives here?' she queried when he ushered her into a lift which whisked them up to a penthouse apartment with panoramic views over the Thames and Westminster.

'I do—although it would be wrong to say that I actually live here. I use the flat as a stopover whenever I'm in London—maybe once or twice a year,' he explained. His phone rang and he glanced at the caller display. 'I need to take this. Feel free to take a look around.'

She couldn't even afford one property, and lived in a

caravan, while he owned a luxury flat in a prime city location and rarely stayed in it! Their lives were worlds apart, Rachel mused as she wandered around the apartment, admiring the elegant décor that was clearly the work of a top interior designer. She paused in the doorway of the master bedroom, her eyes drawn not to the spectacular view across the city but the huge bed in the centre of the room. Tonight Diego would make love to her on that bed. Heat flooded through her veins and she felt the familiar heavy sensation in her pelvis. This was the real reason she had agreed to come away with him, she acknowledged ruefully. Ascot would be a great experience, but she wouldn't care if they missed the racing and spent all their time indulging in a sensual feast. She only had one more week with him before he left for New York, and she was dismayed by the sudden ache in her chest at the knowledge that their affair was almost over. She had always known it would end, but she was unprepared for the sense of panic she felt at the prospect of her life returning to normal—without him.

When she returned to the sitting room, she found Diego chatting to a stunning brunette who looked as though she had stepped from the pages of a fashion journal. Rachel was immediately conscious that her skinny jeans and T-shirt were far from elegant, and she flushed when the woman gave her a speculative glance.

Diego strolled across the room. 'Rachel, I'd like you to meet Jemima Philips. Jemima is a personal stylist and she's going to guide you around the designer boutiques in Mayfair and help you select a few new outfits.'

Rachel stiffened. '*One* new outfit—for Ascot,' she said tightly. 'I don't need anything else.'

'You'll need something to wear to dinner tonight—I've booked a table at Claridge's,' Diego murmured, his mouth curving into a sensual smile that he knew with supreme self-confidence never failed to affect her. 'And of course you will want to buy some lingerie and a few items of smart casual wear as we'll be staying in town for a couple more days.' He noted her frown and dropped a brief tantalising kiss on the mutinous line of her mouth. 'Enjoy it, *querida*,' he bade her, a hint of steel beneath his teasing tone. 'I have a sudden yearning to see you dressed in clothes that flatter your figure rather than swamping it. Most women would jump at the chance to flex my credit card on Bond Street.'

It was on the tip of Rachel's tongue to point out that she was not most women, but his comment that he wanted to see her in flattering clothes stung her pride. He obviously thought she looked a mess in her uniform of jeans or jodhpurs and baggy sweatshirts, and she felt a sudden urge to prove that she could look as elegant as the gorgeous Jemima if she put her mind to it.

But several exhausting hours later, she wished she hadn't taken up Diego's challenge to improve her appearance. Jemima Philips had whisked her around the exclusive boutiques in Bond Street and Sloane Square: Chanel, Gucci, Armani, a boutique specialising in exquisite Italian shoes, and another which sold beautiful and eye-wateringly expensive lingerie. If Rachel had been on her own she would never have had the nerve to walk into any of the shops, and even with Jemima beside her she was horribly conscious of the haughty stares from the sales assistants who cast disdainful glances at her faded jeans. However, the mention of Diego's name seemed to act like a magic wand and the assistants were suddenly gracious and eager to help.

By the end of the day she owned a cream silk dress trimmed with black ribbon and a matching jacket, black stiletto shoes and handbag, and a chic black pillbox hat complete with curled ostrich feathers. Rachel had been determined to pay for her clothes herself, but the bill for her Ascot outfit was so exorbitant that she did not have enough funds in her bank account to cover a fraction of it. Horrified at how much of Diego's money she had spent, she refused to allow Jemima to purchase any of the evening gowns the stylist had nagged her to try on.

After shopping came a visit to a beauty salon favoured by A-list celebrities, where her unruly blonde hair was transformed into a sleek, glossy style with layers around her face and a long sexy fringe. Her face was made up with a range of cosmetics which again cost the earth, but here at least she insisted on paying the bill herself, and as the transaction went through she prayed that her credit limit would not be blown and her card refused.

Diego was waiting at the apartment when a taxi dropped her off. 'You should have had all your purchases delivered, rather than struggling to carry them,' he greeted her when she staggered through the door. When Rachel looked puzzled he indicated several flat boxes emblazoned with the name of the design house on the front. 'Jemima arranged for these to be sent on.'

'It wasn't my choice to buy them,' she muttered when she opened the boxes and discovered the three exquisite evening gowns she had tried on earlier. 'These dresses cost a fortune, Diego, and I can't allow you to buy them for me. I only need one dress for tonight. The other two can be sent back—with all these.' She sifted through the pile of filmy lace bras and knickers in a variety of colours. 'I didn't ask for them. Jemima shouldn't have…'

'Jemima Philips was simply following orders,' he murmured in the honeyed tone he used when he was determined to win an argument. 'You have no idea how beautiful you are, Rachel—but now you will see.' He gave her a gentle push towards the door. 'Go and change into one of the dresses so that I can take you out to dinner. And, Rachel…' She paused and glanced back at him, her heart thudding at the sultry gleam in his eyes. 'Wear the black underwear and the stockings,' he said softly. 'I'm looking forward to removing them later tonight.'

* * *

The following day, Rachel ached all over after Diego had made love to her countless times during a night of the wildest passion they had ever shared. She had read that men were turned on by women wearing stockings and now she knew it was true, she mused, her face growing warm as she recalled his reaction when he had unzipped her evening dress and she had shaken back her hair and posed before him in a sexy black basque, suspenders and stockings.

She'd barely had enough energy to crawl out of bed this morning, but they had left London early to drive to Berkshire and now they were here at one of the most prestigious sporting venues in the world. She turned her head at the sound of hooves thundering along the track and peered through her binoculars as the riders streaked towards the winning post. The racing at Ascot was fantastically exciting, and if she had been down in the main enclosure she would have unashamedly yelled and cheered with the rest of the crowd. But up in the private box, among Diego's wealthy friends, she felt ill at ease and desperate not to draw attention to herself.

She had quickly discovered that this was nigh on impossible when she was the subject of intense speculation among the sophisticated friends of the host of the party, Lord Guy Chetwin.

'Call me Guy,' the aristocratic Englishman had told her when Diego had introduced them. Guy seemed friendly enough—indeed, Rachel had been acutely conscious of his eyes lingering on her several times during lunch—but the other men in the group, and their glamorous socialite wives and girlfriends, were less welcoming and could not hide their curiosity about Diego Ortega's new mistress.

It was a title Rachel felt deeply uncomfortable with—just as she felt unhappy about the fact that every item of clothing she was wearing, and the eye-catching diamond choker Diego had fastened around her throat before they had left the flat this morning, had been paid for by him.

'Your glass is empty. Let's find some more champagne,' Diego murmured in her ear as he led her out onto the balcony, which offered spectacular views of the racetrack.

She forced a smile, but could not dismiss the feeling that she did not belong here. Diego looked utterly gorgeous in full morning dress—a black suit complete with coat-tails, a dove-grey silk waistcoat and tie and a grey top hat which surprisingly did not look odd with his long hair and gave him a rakish air that drew admiring female glances. This rarefied world of the super-rich was his world—but it was not hers. Despite her expensive clothes, she did not fit in with his friends and now that they were away from Hardwick she realised how little she had in common with him.

She glanced back inside and her heart plummeted when she caught sight of a man with a mass of blonde hair flopping onto his brow chatting to Guy Chetwin.

'Jasper Hardwick has just arrived,' she said in a tense whisper as she gripped Diego's arm. 'We'll have to leave. If we walk along the balcony we may be able to slip away without him seeing us.'

'Don't be ridiculous.' Diego frowned. 'I have no intention of leaving. Nor am I going to play a game of hide and seek for the rest of the afternoon. What does it matter if Hardwick sees us?'

'It matters because he'll guess that we're...that we're together,' Rachel snapped. 'And, knowing Jasper, he'll make sure everyone at Hardwick knows. I can't believe he's here,' she muttered.

Diego shrugged. 'He and Guy are old friends. They were at Eton together, although I hadn't realised Hardwick was on the guest list today. I can't believe you're still bothered about our affair being made public,' he added, making no attempt to hide his irritation.

'Doesn't it bother you?' she snapped.

'It has never bothered me, *querida*,' he drawled laconically.

'I respected your wish not to proclaim the fact that we've been sleeping together, but things are different now.'

'How are they?' Rachel demanded, puzzled not just by his statement but the sudden gleam in his eyes.

'Because I want you to come to New York with me next week.'

Diego felt a spurt of satisfaction at her stunned expression. She suddenly looked young and vulnerable, reminding him of the Rachel he had first met rather than the sophisticated woman he had turned her into by buying her designer clothes. When she had walked out of the bedroom this morning, dressed for Ascot, he had been pleased that she looked just as he had wanted her to look, with her hair expertly groomed and her face made-up—her lashes darkened with mascara which emphasised the dense blue of her eyes and her mouth coated in a scarlet gloss. But, for some inexplicable reason, he found that he missed the untidy stable-girl who smelled of the earth and fresh air rather than a cloying, expensive perfume.

It took a few seconds for Diego's words to sink into Rachel's brain, and she felt as shaky as when she had accompanied him across the lawn of the Royal Enclosure in her three-inch stiletto heels. Her heart began to thud erratically. 'To work at your polo school, you mean?' she queried carefully.

'No, *querida*.' His sensual smile stole her breath. 'To pleasure me in bed every night—although we do not have to confine our lovemaking to bed,' he teased wickedly. 'I own a large house in upstate New York, and we could be inventive in the jacuzzi, or on the leather sofa in the sitting room, or maybe I'll spread you across the big walnut desk in my study…'

'Diego…!' She could feel her face burning and was sure they were attracting curious glances from the other guests. But part of her did not care. Diego wanted to extend their affair by taking her to New York, and she was shocked by how tempted she was to say yes. She could not afford to take a break from jumping Piran—not if she was to stand any chance of being selected for the British Equestrian team, she reminded herself urgently. And she couldn't simply disappear from the stables for however long Diego's invitation extended—she noted he had not specified a time limit—and then expect her job to be waiting for her when their affair was over. There was every reason under the sun to refuse him and not one sensible one to accept his invitation, yet it was on the tip of her tongue to agree, to throw caution to the wind and take whatever he was offering for as long as he wanted her.

Dear Lord, she had criticised her mother for leaping into unsuitable relationships with no thought of the consequences, yet here she was, unbearably tempted to do the same thing. She licked her dry lips and forced herself to speak. 'I don't know. I'll have to think about it.'

She would have to think about it? Something kicked in Diego's chest and for a moment he felt faintly incredulous. Never in his life had a woman told him she would have to think about agreeing to continue an affair with him. The situation rarely arose. He had a low boredom threshold and usually tired of his lovers after a few weeks. Rachel was different although, to his intense irritation, he could not work out why she continued to intrigue him. But he had no intention of letting her know that her answer mattered to him. Instead, he closed the gap between them and slid his hand beneath her chin, satisfaction surging through him when he saw the mixture of confusion and undisguised hunger in her cornflower-blue eyes.

'Perhaps this will help you decide,' he murmured as he lowered his head and crushed her soft mouth beneath his. He ignored the fact that he never kissed his lovers in public, intent on bending her to his will in the one way he was certain of victory. She was as stubborn as a mule, and if he was honest he admired her fierce independence. She was a challenge, and perhaps that was why he had not bored of her. All he knew was that he wanted her with him in New York, and from her unguarded response to him he was confident she would agree to come.

When he finally lifted his mouth from hers, Rachel could only stare at him dazedly. Her heart was racing, her face felt hot and she knew her lips must be swollen. So much for wanting to avoid drawing attention to herself, she thought numbly.

'Diego, when you've got a minute, old man, I'd like your tips for the next race,' a voice sounded from behind them.

Diego cast a brief glance at the guest who had interrupted them. 'I'll be right with you, Archie.' He looked down at Rachel's flushed face and smiled. 'Give me your answer tonight,' he murmured. But the triumphant gleam in his eyes when he stepped away from her told her that he was confident of her reply.

With an effort she tore her eyes away from him as he strolled over to a group of his friends, and her heart sank when she saw that Jasper Hardwick had stepped out onto the balcony and was staring at her. Something in his sneering expression made her blood run cold and when a waiter materialised at her side, offering champagne, she took a glass and quickly walked to the far end of the balcony, determined to concentrate on the racing for the remainder of the afternoon.

'What do you think of Ascot, Rachel? I understand this is your first visit.'

She had been standing alone for several minutes when the cultured voice disturbed her solitude. She lowered her binoculars and smiled hesitantly at Guy Chetwin. 'It is. And it's…' she gave a faint shrug, her glance encompassing the view of the crowds in the public enclosure below, the velvet green lawns and the racing track that sliced through the grounds like an emerald river '…spectacular.'

'I'm glad you are enjoying the day.' Guy moved until he was standing a little too close for Rachel's liking. His thin mouth curved into a smile, but the eyes that trailed slowly over her were coolly assessing. 'You look charming, my dear. Diego has always had exceptionally good taste.'

Guy made her sound like an object rather than a person. Something in his tone caused Rachel to stiffen and her hand moved unconsciously to the diamond choker around her neck.

His eyes followed her movement. 'A pretty trinket,' he commented. 'Cartier, if I'm not mistaken?'

'I believe so,' she murmured. 'Diego gave it to me.' She was going to add that she had only reluctantly agreed to wear the necklace to Ascot after intense persuasion from Diego, but Guy spoke first.

'I'm sure you deserve it.' He uttered the curious statement in a pleasant enough tone, but Rachel detected a nuance in his voice that made her skin crawl. 'I hear you're accompanying Diego to New York.'

'How do you know…?' She struggled to hide her shock that Diego must have discussed her with his friend. 'Actually, I haven't decided whether to go yet.'

'Ah…' Guy laughed. 'Well, I don't blame you for trying to up the stakes. But a word of advice, my dear. Don't keep him dangling for too long. There are plenty of other pretty penniless young women who attend events such as Ascot with the sole intention of bagging themselves a rich lover.'

This time the edge of contempt in his voice was unmistakable and Rachel flushed. 'I'm not with Diego because he's wealthy,' she said tightly.

'Of course you are,' Guy drawled in a coldly amused tone. 'I can spot a common little gold-digger a mile off.' He lifted his hand to her throat and traced his finger over the diamond choker. 'I see that you have expensive tastes, but you are quite clearly not one of us. Diego might have dressed you in haute couture, but I'm afraid nothing can disguise your lack of breeding,' he added bluntly.

Humiliation engulfed Rachel, robbing her of a reply to Guy's outrageous comments. A cheer went up as the leading horse on the track swept past the finishing post. The sun was blazing in the cloudless sky but she felt icy cold and she gripped the balcony rail as Guy moved away from her and melted into the crowd who had spilled out of the box to watch the race. Part of her wanted to follow him and demand an apology for his disgusting suggestion that she was a gold-digger but, as she stared down at her designer dress and her hand strayed once more to the diamonds around her neck, her stomach lurched with the realisation that, by accepting Diego's gifts of clothes and jewellery, she had sold herself to him.

Last night's sex had been amazing but she had been aware of a subtle change in his attitude towards her—a new boldness in his demands and an expectation for her to fulfil his every fantasy. She had felt flattered that he was so turned on by her wearing her new sexy underwear, but now she wondered sickly if he believed he had paid for her to please him.

What had happened to her fiercely guarded independence? she wondered, fighting the nausea that swept through her. How could she have sacrificed it for a sexual liaison that she had known from the outset would never mean anything to Diego? The trials for the British showjumping team were coming up and she should be spending all her free time practising on Piran, but instead she had been on the brink of agreeing to take off to New York with a man who had never given any indication that she meant anything to him outside the bedroom.

Rachel bit her lip and forced herself to face the truth. The reason she had been contemplating going with him was because she had hoped that their affair would develop into something deeper—that Diego would fall for her as she had fallen for him. Ever since he had invited her to Ascot she had been kidding herself that there must be a reason why he wanted to introduce her to his friends. And when he had asked her to accompany him to New York she had taken it as proof that he was starting to feel something for her and regarded her as more than a casual sex partner.

Guy Chetwin's scathing comment that she was 'not one of

us' made her realise what a fool she had been. Diego would never want more than a brief affair with her. The social divide between them was enormous, but it was not just that—it was Diego himself. At this moment he was chatting and laughing with the other guests, drawing people to him with his effortless charm. But she recognised that he was essentially a loner who guarded his emotions and never allowed anyone too close. In all the time they had spent together, he had never spoken of his family and had steered their conversation firmly away from his personal life. She did not really know him at all, she realised miserably.

Lost in a sea of dark thoughts, she was unaware that he had joined her until his deep-timbred voice sent the familiar quiver down her spine.

'You are cold, *querida*,' he murmured, running his hand lightly over her arm and noting the tiny goose bumps on her skin. 'Shall we go inside? Jasper Hardwick has gone down to the Royal Enclosure, by the way.' He frowned when Rachel made no acknowledgement of his presence. 'You seemed to be getting on well with Guy,' he said lightly, irritated with himself for the ridiculous spurt of jealousy he'd felt when he had watched them standing close together. 'What were you talking about?'

Rachel gave a brittle laugh. 'Your friend Guy accused me of being a gold-digger,' she said tightly. 'He believes I'm only with you because I want to get my grubby hands on your money.'

Diego's eyes narrowed on her angry face. 'I'm sure you must have been mistaken…' he began slowly.

'I wasn't,' Rachel interrupted him fiercely. 'According to Lord Chetwin, Ascot is a popular hunting ground for pretty penniless women who are looking for a rich stud. He thinks I sold myself to you. And that's what you think too, isn't it, Diego?' she demanded shrilly, hurt and humiliation threatening to shatter her tenuous grip on her self-control. 'The clothes and the necklace—they were payment for my "services".'

'I do not regard them as *payment* for anything,' he growled. 'You needed something to wear today…'

'So that I would be socially acceptable to your wealthy friends,' Rachel said bitterly. 'But apparently the posh frock and the diamonds don't disguise my lack of breeding.'

Her voice had risen once again. Diego frowned when heads turned in their direction. 'This is ridiculous,' he snapped. 'There has clearly been a misunderstanding. I'll find Guy and explain that you are my…'

He hesitated, and in the tense silence that quivered between them Rachel's stomach churned. 'Your what, Diego?' she asked huskily. 'Perhaps this is a good time to clarify our relationship…and discuss our future.'

Diego stiffened. The conversation was sounding ominously like the ones he'd had with previous lovers, when the word *commitment* reared its ugly head. His dark brows winged upwards. 'Our future, *querida*?' he said in a dangerously soft tone. 'I'm afraid there is little to discuss.'

'Then why did you ask me to go to New York with you?' In her heart she knew the answer, but she needed to have it spelled out. 'Was it really just for sex?'

Yes, damn it, he thought furiously. He wasn't prepared to admit to himself, let alone to Rachel, that he had been looking forward to showing her around one of his favourite cities.

'Don't knock it, Rachel,' he said coldly. 'I haven't heard you complaining. You've enjoyed our affair as much as I have. I thought we could continue to enjoy each other for another month while I'm in the States, but to be frank, I never considered that it would lead to any kind of permanent arrangement.'

Rachel tried to ignore the tearing pain in her chest. 'I see,' she said quietly.

'*Dios!*' he growled harshly, infuriated by the note of hurt in her voice, and by the unexpected feeling of guilt that tugged at his insides. 'I made it clear from the start that I'm not in the market for any kind of committed relationship.' If it was emotion she was looking for, she had come to the wrong man—because his had died with Eduardo. He was cold and empty inside, but in a strange way he welcomed the aching loneliness. It was what he deserved—a punishment and a pain that would last a lifetime.

'I thought you were happy with a no-strings affair,' he said tersely. His frustration bubbled over. 'What were you expecting, Rachel—a marriage proposal?'

'Of course not,' she snapped, stung by his scathing tone. 'But, to go to New York with you, I would have to give up my job, my financial security, and probably my dreams of winning a place in the British Equestrian team. That's a lot to ask of me, Diego, when all you're offering in return is a month in your bed.'

Honesty forced Diego to acknowledge the truth of her words, but he was furious that she had backed him into a corner. Rachel's message was clear—commit to some sort of relationship or I won't come to the States with you. Fine, he thought grimly. He'd never been dictated to by a woman in his life, and he wasn't going to start now.

'But that's all I am offering, *querida*,' he said coldly. 'Take it or leave it.'

Rachel was unprepared for the surge of pain that swept through her. This was it. It was over—the ending of their affair as sudden and unexpected as its beginning. It didn't have to be the end, a voice whispered urgently in her head. She could smile and shake back her hair—look him boldly in the eyes and agree to his terms. Fantastic sex with no emotions involved for another month. But emotions *were* involved, she acknowledged heavily. Her emotions. She was falling in love with him—and she had to end it now, before her heart suffered serious damage. She was not like her mother. She would not sacrifice everything for a man. Not even this man.

Tears burned the back of her throat but she would rather die than cry in front of him. 'I'll leave it,' she told him, proud that she sounded strong and in control when she felt anything but. 'And I think it would be best if I leave immediately—before any of your other friends accuse me of being a gold-digger,' she added bitterly.

'I'll speak to Guy,' Diego said tersely. 'I have no doubt he'll be anxious to apologise for his mistake.'

'Forget it,' Rachel said dully, suddenly bone weary. 'I don't care what he thinks of me. I just want to go.'

Diego stiffened. If she thought he would beg and plead, she was mistaken. His eyes narrowed on her delicate face and he remembered how she had writhed beneath him last night, her cheeks flushed and her mouth reddened and swollen from his kisses. She was beautiful, and he could not deny that he desired her. But beautiful women were ten-a-penny, he reminded himself grimly, and desire was transitory.

'Very well. I intend to enjoy the rest of the day's racing, but I'll arrange for a chauffeur to take you back to London.' Perhaps a couple of hours on her own would bring her to her senses, he brooded sardonically. After a cooling off period he was confident she would change her mind. The sexual alchemy between them was too intense for either of them to walk away until it had burned itself out. 'We'll spend tonight at the flat and I'll drive you back to Gloucestershire tomorrow.' He swung on his heel and strode off, but then paused and glanced back at her motionless figure. 'Come with me now,' he ordered impatiently. 'I'll escort you to the car.'

CHAPTER SEVEN

'I'LL see you later,' Diego told Rachel brusquely as he shut the car door. When the limousine pulled away she turned her head and stared back at him, desperate to imprint his face on her mind one last time—because she had no intention of being at the flat when he returned.

Back in London, it took her less than twenty minutes to change into her jeans, hang up her Ascot outfit in the wardrobe with the other clothes Diego had bought her, and place the diamond choker back in its velvet box. By the time he walked into the penthouse and discovered it empty, she was at Paddington Station, boarding a train to Gloucester.

Rachel spent the following few days on tenterhooks, waiting for Diego to return to Hardwick, certain that he would be furious with her for running out on him. She had made it clear that she was ending their affair, but could she trust herself to resist him if he tried to persuade her back into his bed?

In the event her sleepless nights were for nothing. Diego was due to spend one more week at Hardwick Polo Club, but on Monday morning, when she arrived at the stables, she learned from the other stable-hands that he wasn't coming back and had already flown to his polo school in the States.

'How was your trip to Cornwall?' Alex asked her.

'Cornwall…?' She stared at him blankly, her insides churning at the knowledge that Diego had gone and that she would never see him again.

'To see your dad—Diego told us you'd gone to visit him for a few days,' Alex said cheerfully.

'Oh…yes…it was fine,' she mumbled, shaken that Diego had lied on her behalf. He had known she hadn't wanted anyone at Hardwick to find out about their affair and the re-alisation that he had taken steps to protect her from being the subject of gossip caused her heart to splinter.

She had done the right thing in refusing to go to New York with him, she reassured herself that night as she tossed restlessly beneath the sheet, unable to sleep in her airless caravan. In a few weeks' time Diego would return to his native Argentina—and she would have had to come back to England and start all over again, looking for a job and somewhere to live. Another month in his bed was all he had ever offered, and she would never forget the hard expression in his eyes when he'd challenged her to 'take it or leave it'.

The days after she had ended her affair with Diego stretched slowly into weeks, and eventually the whole summer dragged by, but the curious lethargy that had settled over Rachel grew steadily worse. Life seemed to have lost its sparkle, and the aching loneliness inside her was not eased by spending time with her friends, or even riding Piran. She seemed to be running on autopilot and even though she threw herself into work and socialising, and competing in various showjump-ing events, nothing could alter the fact that she missed Diego desperately.

In early September she won a place with the British Show Jumping Team to compete in the European championships. Peter Irving was delighted and she forced herself to act as though she was excited. Competing at a national level had been her lifelong ambition, but instead of feeling euphoric she felt flat and tired, and angry with herself that she was still pining for a man who had probably forgotten all about her.

Diego had been busy for the past weeks. Rachel had read in various riding magazines of his success in polo matches in Barbados, Singapore, and most recently at the US Open Polo Championships in Palm Beach, Florida, and she had felt sick with misery when she'd stared at the photo of him surrounded by gorgeous glamour models. The nauseous feeling continued to plague her. She'd probably picked up one of the many viruses that seemed to be around in the autumn, but decided to mention it to her doctor when she went to collect a new supply of her contraceptive pill.

'Everything else is normal?' the doctor queried. 'When was your last period?'

Rachel frowned. Since she had been on the pill her periods were so light that they often only lasted for a day and she never made a note of them. Her last pill-free week had been three weeks ago, but now that she thought of it, she could not recall needing to buy tampons for ages.

'I think I might have missed a couple,' she said slowly, puzzled rather than concerned. 'But the same thing happened last year, and it turned out that I was anaemic.'

'Well, I can arrange a blood test. And it might be an idea to do a pregnancy test—just to rule it out,' the doctor murmured when she caught Rachel's shocked expression.

'I *can't* be pregnant,' she said forcefully. 'I've never, ever forgotten to take a pill.'

She repeated the statement to the surgery nurse when she handed in her urine sample. 'I'm sure there's nothing to worry about,' the nurse replied soothingly. 'Take a seat in the waiting room and the doctor will call you in to discuss the result in a few minutes.'

Rachel tried to ignore the nervous flutter in her stomach. Of course she wasn't pregnant. She'd lost weight over the past weeks rather than gained it and was thinner than ever. It was true that she was more tired than usual, and had been for weeks, but that wasn't surprising when she had been sleeping badly—her dreams regularly haunted by Diego.

It was just a blip in her cycle, she reassured herself. But the grave expression on the doctor's face when she walked into the consulting room filled her with dread.

'It must be a mistake,' she croaked minutes later, so utterly devastated by the news that she was expecting Diego's baby that she could barely speak.

'Did you have a stomach upset at any time?' the doctor queried. 'Being sick can reduce the effectiveness of the pill— as can certain antibiotics.'

Rachel shook her head but the reference to antibiotics triggered a memory. 'I was bitten by a horse,' she said slowly, 'and at the casualty unit I was given a course of antibiotics to prevent the wound infecting. That couldn't have led to me falling pregnant—could it?' she asked desperately.

'I'll check with the hospital to see which antibiotics you were given, but it's the most likely reason. More important is the fact that you are definitely pregnant, and I'm going to arrange for you to have a scan to determine when you conceived.'

When you conceived… The words thudded in Rachel's brain. It was now the end of September, and she had ended her affair with Diego on Ladies' Day at Ascot, which this year had been the nineteenth of June. That meant that she must be nearly four months pregnant—possibly more, she thought sickly, remembering how she had been bitten by Earl Hardwick's horse and started the course of antibiotics on the day after she had made love with Diego for the first time.

'I don't look pregnant,' she said desperately, staring down at her flat stomach.

'A scan will tell us more,' the doctor said firmly.

And it did. Four days later Rachel stared disbelievingly at

the grainy image on the screen while the nurse pointed out her baby's heartbeat and explained that she was eighteen weeks pregnant.

'The baby is only six inches long at the moment. There's plenty of time for you—and he or she—to grow,' the nurse said cheerfully when Rachel—still clinging to the forlorn hope that it could all be a mistake—pointed out that she did not have a bump or any other visible signs that she was pregnant.

How hadn't she known? she wondered as she lay in bed in the caravan that night, her mind whirling. She felt as though her body had let her down by withholding the usual signs of pregnancy. But the signs had been there, she acknowledged grimly. It was just that she'd put her uncharacteristic tiredness and mood swings down to the fact that she was in love with a man who lived on the other side of the world and wanted nothing more to do with her.

The doctor had told her that taking the pill during the early stages of her pregnancy would not have harmed the baby. She had also quietly pointed out to Rachel that if she did not wish to continue with the pregnancy they would have to act fast. Rachel's response had been immediate—she could not contemplate a termination—but she felt neither joy nor excitement at the prospect of having a child.

'Tell the father, and give his name to the Child Support Agency if he refuses to cough up with some money,' her mother advised when, in sheer desperation, Rachel phoned her. 'Bringing up a kid alone is tough, I can tell you.'

Liz Summers could offer no practical help. She had left her third husband for an Irish artist and was moving to Dublin, taking Rachel's twin half-sisters with her, and she had made it clear that she did not view the prospect of being a grandmother with any enthusiasm. Rachel shuddered at the idea of asking Diego for money. She did not want anything from him, but he had the right to know that she was expecting his child, she acknowledged heavily. The only trouble was she had no idea how to contact him. She knew he owned a ranch, but Argentina was a big country.

Eventually her brain clicked into gear and she found the number of his polo school in New York on the Internet but, when she phoned, the receptionist refused to give his address in Argentina, and instead took Rachel's name and promised she would pass on the message for him to phone her. But he didn't ring, and as the weeks passed Rachel stopped rehearsing how she would break the news that she was expecting his baby and faced up to the fact that she was five months pregnant; she would not be able to continue with her job at the stables for much longer—or keep her place with the British Show Jumping Team—and that a cramped caravan was not a suitable place to bring up a child.

It was raining in Gloucestershire—sheeting rain that teemed down the car windscreen faster than the wipers could clear it. Diego's mouth compressed as he negotiated the winding lanes leading to Hardwick Hall, and not for the first time he wondered what he was doing here when he could be on a plane to Argentina.

He had recently been in Thailand, competing in a series of polo matches, and he missed the heat and sunshine. Back home, the temperature in Buenos Aires would be thirty degrees centigrade, but here in England the display on the car dashboard was registering a measly three degrees and the late November sky was a dismal slate grey. A series of business meetings in London had necessitated him staying at his Thames-side apartment for the past couple of weeks, evoking memories of the last time he had been there with Rachel, and his curiosity to know why she had tried to contact him had finally got the better of him.

He drove straight past the entrance to the Hardwick estate. The groom he'd spoken to when he had phoned the stables had explained that Rachel no longer worked there, but that she was still living in the caravan on Irving's farm. Why had she left Hardwick and the job he knew she loved? he brooded. And where did she now keep her horse?

Diego frowned, irritated with himself for his interest. From the moment he'd walked into his apartment after the day at Ascot and found her gone, he had dismissed her from his mind, furious—and, if he was honest, piqued—that she had been the one to end their affair. It was a novelty he had not enjoyed and he'd felt a certain amount of satisfaction when the receptionist at his polo school in New York had passed on a message that a Miss Rachel Summers had requested that he should phone her.

It was almost two months since Rachel had tried to contact him, and he had been too busy travelling to polo competitions around the world to return her call. But, to his annoyance, she had lurked in his subconscious. Had she called because she wanted to resume their affair? He was about to find out, Diego thought grimly as he drove through the farmyard and up the muddy track.

The caravan looked even smaller and older than he remembered. Maybe she had decided that being the mistress of a multimillionaire wasn't so bad after all, he brooded cynically. Not that he had any intention of taking her back. But, to his intense irritation, he could not control the sudden quickening of his heartbeat as he walked up the caravan steps and rapped on the door.

'Hello, Rachel.'

Rachel was suffering from a flu virus. For the past three days she'd had a pounding headache, a sore throat and aching limbs, and her temperature must be sky high, because now she was hallucinating.

'Diego?'

She could barely comprehend that he was here, and she was horrified by the effect his sudden appearance was having on her. Her heart was pounding and she felt breathless and dizzy, but none of these symptoms were the result of her pregnancy—or the flu virus, she acknowledged dismally.

The sight of him after all this time seared her soul. He was even more gorgeous than she remembered, his tanned skin gleaming like polished bronze and his silky dark hair brushing his shoulders. She wanted to touch him, felt a desperate urge to throw herself against his chest and have him close his arms around her and hold her safe. But when had she ever been safe with Diego? she asked herself bitterly. He was the reason that every one of her dreams had turned to dust.

'What do you want?' she croaked.

Diego frowned and glanced over her shoulder at the packing boxes and the pile of clothes that littered the floor. 'To talk to you,' he said tersely. 'Can I come in? This is obviously a bad time, but I'm flying home tomorrow.'

The last thing Rachel wanted to do was invite Diego into her caravan, and their 'talk' was likely to be explosive, she thought grimly, but the rain was soaking his hair and shoulders and dully she stepped back to allow him inside. It was amazing how much clutter she'd collected over the last five years, she thought ruefully, hastily shifting a pile of old riding magazines so that he could sit down.

Even sitting, Diego seemed to dominate the tiny living space. He stretched his long legs out in front of him and Rachel felt a fierce tug of longing as her eyes skimmed his black designer jeans and the superbly cut tan leather jacket that he wore over a black fine-knit sweater. He looked as incongruous as he had done the first time he had visited her caravan and, as she recalled the passion that had flamed between them on that occasion, colour flooded her pale cheeks.

But there was no hint of the feverish desire that had burned in his amber eyes that day. He was looking at her with an expression of faint distaste that grew more marked as his gaze moved down from her lank hair, scraped back in a ponytail, to her voluminous sweatshirt. His eyes were cold and hard.

Rachel had forgotten how autocratic he could look and she was suddenly glad that the sweatshirt concealed the still quite small bump of her pregnancy.

'Why are you here?' she mumbled, her voice thick with cold.

'I received the message you left with the Ortega Academy in New York that you wanted to speak to me,' Diego replied laconically. 'Was it something important?'

Rachel gave a harsh laugh, her temper flaring at his patent disinterest. 'Do you care if it was? I called you two months ago.'

His eyes narrowed at the accusation in her voice. 'I've been busy.'

She recalled the newspaper photo of him surrounded by the promotional models and felt sick. 'Yes, I imagine you have.'

'From the look of it, so have you,' Diego commented, glancing at the packing boxes. 'Can I take it you've finally decided to move to somewhere more habitable?'

'There's nothing wrong with living in a caravan,' Rachel said tightly, infuriated by his scathing tone. 'It's just that it's not a suitable place to bring up a baby…'

Every muscle in Diego's body tensed. His heart had frozen into a solid block of ice on the day Eduardo had died, and he had believed that nothing could ever touch him or stir his emotions. Now, as a torrent of feelings swept through him, he realised that he had been wrong. He was astounded by Rachel's startling statement but, to his surprise, his over-whelming reaction to the news that she was carrying another man's child was one of gut-wrenching disappointment.

The silence between them simmered with tension. This was not how Rachel had ever envisaged telling Diego that she was expecting his baby, she acknowledged wryly. The words had spilled out of her mouth and the moment she'd uttered them she'd stiffened, waiting fearfully for his reaction. His expression was unfathomable, but after a few moments he gave a faint shrug and got to his feet.

'I see,' he murmured coldly. 'Well, I think that's my cue to leave.' He turned towards the door but then glanced back at her, his lip curling in a look of utter contempt. 'You didn't waste much time hopping into another man's bed, did you, Rachel? Who is the father, by the way—your red-haired stable-boy? Tell me, did you get together with him after you walked out on me, or were you sleeping with both of us at the same time?'

Rachel flinched at his deliberate crudity and a curious numbness seeped through her body. She had never kidded herself that Diego would welcome the news of her pregnancy, but he was looking at her as though she was the lowest life-form on the planet. She licked her suddenly dry lips and forced her throat to work. 'It's not Alex's baby,' she said quietly. 'It's yours.'

Anger coursed through Diego's veins like molten lava. What kind of a fool did she take him for? 'How can you possibly be carrying my child when we split up months ago? If your boyfriend won't face up to his responsibilities, that's your problem. It has nothing to do with me.'

Rachel had been so shocked by Diego's furious denial that he was the father of her baby that her brain temporarily ceased functioning. But, as he pulled open the door and she realised he was actually going to leave, she jerked back to life. Anger burned inside her, turning the ice in her blood to fire. Trembling with rage, she gripped the hem of her sweatshirt and dragged it over her head, and felt a swift spurt of satis-faction at the undisguised shock in his eyes when he stared at her swollen stomach.

'This is your baby, Diego,' she said fiercely. 'I'm seven months pregnant. I didn't even know until I was almost five months, and when I found out, I tried to contact you. I thought you had a right to know.'

Diego shook his head, his eyes glacial. 'I don't believe for a second that I'm the father. And if you think I'm going to pay out for another man's child, think again.'

'Alex is my friend. We have never been lovers,' Rachel cried angrily.

Diego threw her another look of withering scorn and strode down the caravan steps. 'Then you must have trapped some other poor fool,' he snarled. 'But I tell you now, *querida*, you're not dragging me into your web of deceit.'

He was going—marching across the field and leaving footprints in the mud. Rachel stared disbelievingly at his retreating form and for a few seconds she thought—let him go and good riddance. But then the baby kicked and she automatically put her hand on her stomach and felt the hard bulge of a tiny foot or elbow. It wasn't the baby's fault that it had been conceived by sheer fluke. Yet Diego had turned his back on his child, had utterly rejected the possibility that he was the father. Anger surged through her once more and she gripped the edge of the door frame, peering through at the rain that fell relentlessly from the leaden sky.

'You are the father, Diego. It couldn't be anyone else because you're the only man I've ever slept with.'

He carried on walking without altering his pace, but then halted abruptly and swung back to stare at her, his face as cold and hard as if he had been hewn from granite. 'What did you say?' he queried in a dangerously soft tone.

'The first time we made love…I was a virgin,' she faltered.

'Liar.' The single word cracked through the air like a gunshot. 'I would have known,' he added arrogantly before he swung on his heel and disappeared down the track.

CHAPTER EIGHT

RACHEL was lying. She had to be. He had not been her first lover. Diego stared moodily out of the hotel window at the wintry landscape. He hated England at this time of year—cold, grey and as dismal as his spirits. He was due to catch a flight to Buenos Aires later today and he was impatient to be on his way but, to his fury, he could not forget the image of her standing in the doorway of her dilapidated caravan, crying out to him that he was the father of her child.

The waitress who had served him at dinner last night sashayed over to his table and smiled at him. He noted that she had unfastened the top three buttons of her blouse, and when she took out her pad to take his order she deliberately leaned close to him.

'Would you like the full English breakfast, Mr Ortega? Bacon, sausage, egg, fried bread...'

Diego's stomach churned. He hadn't slept last night and this morning his appetite was non-existent. 'I'll just have more coffee, thank you.'

'Are you staying long?' The waitress looked at him guilelessly from beneath her lashes. 'I could always show you around, if you like.'

The girl was pretty and blonde, and eight months ago he would probably have been sufficiently interested to take up her offer. Now, all he could think of was another blonde with big cornflower-blue eyes that had watched him when she'd thought he hadn't noticed.

When he had first arrived at Hardwick, Rachel had been feisty and hot-tempered, but she had also been shy and wary and had gone to great lengths to hide her awareness of him. She had responded to him when he had kissed her with a passion that had inflamed his desire, but when he had taken her to bed that first time he had been faintly surprised by her hesitancy, he recalled grimly.

Santa Madre! Was it possible he had taken her virginity that night? And, in return, had he given her a child? He frowned, remembering his frustration when he'd realised he did not have any protection—and the sweet flood of relief when she had assured him she was on the pill. He had been so hungry for her that he had ignored the voice of common sense in his head reminding him of his golden rule that contraception was his responsibility.

Clearly she had lied to him, but it did not necessarily follow that he was the father of her baby, he reminded himself darkly. She could have had other lovers after him. It was possible that she was less than seven months pregnant. But as he pictured her swollen belly, clearly outlined beneath the clingy top she had been wearing under her sweatshirt yesterday, he acknowledged with a heavy sense of finality that her pregnancy was well advanced.

Anger coursed through him—directed as much at his own stupidity as Rachel's duplicity. He would demand proof that the child was his before he paid her a penny—because of course money was what she wanted. And then he would… what? Walk away? Could he really go back to Argentina and get on with his life, knowing that his own flesh and blood was being brought up in a field? He did not want a child, and yet if Rachel was to be believed his child would come into this world in a matter of weeks. A mixture of frustration and fury gnawed in his gut, but at the same time he could not deny a sense of wonderment at the idea of being a father.

Diego had no memory of his own father. According to his mother, Ricardo had left her for some harlot he'd picked up in Buenos Aires when he and Eduardo were babies. Lorena Ortega had married a good-for-nothing gigolo—a fact that Diego's grandfather had frequently pointed out, before adding in the same breath that Diego was just like his father.

He could almost hear the old man now, taunting him that he was a feckless, unreliable playboy. Such was Alonso Ortega's hatred of his son-in-law that after Lorena had divorced Ricardo Hernandez she had abided by her father's wishes and changed her name, and that of her two sons, back to Ortega. Alonso would not have been surprised that Diego had fathered an illegitimate child. Like father, like son, he would have decreed, had he still been alive. But his grandfather would have been wrong, Diego thought fiercely, pushing his half-drunk cup of coffee aside and jerking to his feet. If he really was the father of Rachel's baby, then he would accept his responsibilities and do what needed to be done.

Moving house was stressful at the best of times, and Rachel had discovered that moving, after spending the previous night alternating between rage and tears after her confrontation with Diego, and with a soaring temperature and a throat that felt as though she'd swallowed broken glass had sent her stress levels through the roof.

Not that she had actually moved into a house, she acknowledged as she stared around the shabby bedsit on the top floor of the Rose and Crown. But the room was marginally bigger and warmer than the caravan, and she was grateful to Bill Bailey, the landlord, for offering it to her for a very reasonable rent.

Thanks to Bill, she also had a job working as a waitress in the pub's restaurant, at least until the baby came. Being on her feet for hours every evening made her legs and back ache, but since she could no longer ride she could not afford to be choosy about where she worked. Job opportunities for an unmarried pregnant stable-hand were not exactly thick on the ground, she thought ruefully. Since she had left Hardwick Polo Club the news of her pregnancy had flown around the village, and speculation that Diego Ortega was the father of her baby had been fuelled by Jasper Hardwick.

What she was going to do when the baby was born, she had no idea. Earl Hardwick had said he would abide by the terms of her employment contract and keep a job for her at the polo club, but in reality she knew she could not return to work at the stables when she had a baby to care for and her low wages would not cover child-care fees. She was struggling to survive now on the small amount of maternity pay she was entitled to, and without Bill's kindness she did not know how she would manage.

The future was beginning to loom frighteningly close when she considered that she was due to give birth in the middle of February and it was already late November. One thing was certain—she would have to manage on her own, she thought grimly. Diego had made it abundantly clear that he wanted nothing to do with her, or the baby that he refused to believe was his.

She sat on the edge of the bed and glanced wearily at the boxes that Bill had carried up the three flights of stairs to the attic flat. She really should start to unpack, but she was so cold that her teeth were chattering and she curled up in a ball, dragged the duvet over her and fell instantly into a restless doze.

Even while she was asleep her head was pounding. The insistent hammering was going right through her brain, but then suddenly, blessedly it stopped.

'So you *are* here—the landlord said you were in. I've been knocking for five minutes. Why didn't you open the door?'

Rachel winced as the angry growl penetrated her skull, and she forced her eyes open and peered groggily at Diego. 'What are *you* doing here?' Her voice sounded over-loud in her ears—she was unaware that it had emerged from her raw throat as a hoarse whisper.

There was a frown of concern on Diego's face as he hunkered down next to the bed and placed his hand on her brow. '*Dios*, you're burning up with a fever,' he muttered. 'Don't go back to sleep, Rachel; I need to get you to a doctor.'

'I saw my doctor two days ago,' she told him, fighting her way out of the duvet because she was now boiling over. 'I've just got a flu virus, that's all, but I can't take any of the usual cold remedies because of the baby.'

The mere mention of the baby caused Diego's brows to lower ominously—although, even when he looked angry, he was still the most gorgeous man she'd ever set eyes on, Rachel thought bleakly. Today he was wearing pale denim jeans and a thick oatmeal sweater topped by a suede car-coat, and he looked so powerful and ruggedly good-looking that her insides melted. She pushed the duvet aside and as his eyes skimmed over her she felt horribly self-conscious of her stomach, clearly defined beneath her maternity top.

'What do you want?' she demanded tersely.

God alone knew—because he certainly didn't, Diego thought grimly. All he knew was that the sight of Rachel looking so heart-wrenchingly vulnerable evoked a curious ache in his chest. He forced himself to ignore it and stood up, no flicker of warmth in his amber eyes as he stared down at her.

'I want the truth,' he said harshly, his accent sounding very pronounced. 'I will ask you one more time. Who is the father of your child?'

'You can ask me a hundred times and the answer will still be the same,' Rachel snapped. How dared he doubt her word? She glared at him, stiff with pride and anger, unaware of how fragile she looked with her hair spilling around her shoulders and the hectic, unhealthy flush on her cheeks. 'You are.'

Diego's jaw clenched as bitter anger swirled inside him.

Anger at himself for having been such a gullible fool, and anger at her for…for walking out on him, he owned grimly. He had felt as though he'd been kicked in the gut when he had returned to his London apartment after Ascot and found she'd gone. And now, months later, she was insisting that her body was swollen with his child. 'I want proof,' he said icily. 'I did some research last night and discovered that it's now possible to run a DNA test while a child is in the womb. You'll have to give a blood sample, and from that the baby's DNA can be detected with no risk to either of you.'

'I don't need to prove anything,' Rachel snapped furiously. 'You were the first and only man I've ever had sex with and, like it or not, this baby is yours.'

An unexpected surge of possessiveness swept through Diego at the idea that he was Rachel's only lover. She could be lying, but he could not dismiss his memory of her rapt expression that first time he had made love to her, the look of startled wonder in her eyes when he had eased into her and joined their bodies as one. But, if she had been a virgin, why hadn't she told him?

'Did you plan to get pregnant?' he growled angrily.

Rachel was so shocked by his accusation that for a moment she could not speak. 'Did I *plan* it?' she said in a tight, cold voice. 'Do you think I *want* to be pregnant?' Blinding, burning rage swept through her. 'I have lost everything,' she told him bitterly. 'The job that I loved, my home—my horse.' She swallowed the lump that formed in her throat every time she thought of Piran. 'I had won a place with the British Show Jumping Team, but obviously I had to stand down.' Her voice faltered. 'I couldn't deprive Piran of his chance to compete in the European Championships, and fortunately Peter Irving managed to find another rider to take my place. Piran now lives on his new owner's farm in Norfolk—too far away for me to visit him,' she said thickly.

She closed her eyes wearily, blocking out Diego's startled

expression. 'No, I didn't plan it, and I didn't lie to you. I was on the pill but it didn't work properly—something to do with the antibiotics I was prescribed after I was bitten by that horse. It was just…bad luck,' she said quietly. 'But it's my problem, Diego, and I'll deal with it. I don't want anything from you. I'll manage fine on my own.'

Diego's brows drew together. The conversation wasn't going as he had envisaged. He had expected Rachel to be pleased to see him, grateful that he had given her another chance to convince him that he was the baby's father. And he *was* convinced, he realised with a jolt. Even without a DNA test, his instincts told him that the child she was carrying was his—but, instead of seeming pleased that he was here, she was prickly and belligerent, and plainly unhappy about being pregnant.

His eyes were drawn to her swollen stomach and he felt a curious sensation in his chest, as if his heart were expanding. His child was growing inside her. If she was seven months along, then the baby must be fully formed—his son or daughter, and the next Ortega heir. He felt an overwhelming urge to reach out and touch Rachel's abdomen, to feel his child move. But something in her angry stare warned him that she would not allow him the liberty of touching her, not when there was this yawning chasm of mistrust between them.

'How do you intend to manage?' he queried, glancing around the shabby room with its collection of old furniture and wallpaper peeling in places from the walls.

Rachel moved over to the window and looked down on the paved back yard where the pub guard dogs—two massive black Rottweilers—were prowling. She certainly wouldn't be able to put the baby outside in the pram for some fresh air, she thought ruefully. It was yet another reminder that her situation was far from ideal.

'I'm thinking about having the baby adopted.'

For the second time in his life Diego felt as though he had been kicked in the stomach. Discovering that he was going to be a father had been shocking enough, but Rachel's calm statement sent the oxygen rushing from his lungs. 'How could you even contemplate such a thing?' he grated savagely. 'Do you think I would allow you to hand my child over to strangers?'

Something pinged in Rachel's chest at the possessive way Diego had said 'my child', and for the first time since her pregnancy had been confirmed she pictured the baby as a little human being rather than an alien growing inside her and altering her body-shape out of recognition. Up until now she had viewed her unplanned pregnancy as a problem—a huge life-changing problem that she felt ill-equipped to deal with. But now, suddenly, she was intrigued by the little person that she and Diego had created. Was the baby a boy, with dark hair and his father's tiger-like amber eyes? she wondered. And could she really give birth to this baby and then give it away?

Diego was staring at her as if she were a despicable mass murderer, and she knew she sounded defensive when she snapped, '*Your* child, Diego? Yesterday you were adamant that the baby's father was one of my legions of lovers.'

'And today I am prepared to accept the likelihood that the child is mine,' he bit back tersely. He shook his head, utterly taken aback by the idea that she did not intend to keep the baby. What kind of life would this child have, he wondered grimly, deprived of that most fundamental requirement—a mother's love? He knew what that felt like. From as far back as he could remember, his mother had disliked him and had reserved all her love for Eduardo. His grandmother had told him before she had died that his birth had taken everyone by surprise. His mother had not known she was expecting twins and his arrival into the world had been a traumatic experience for her after Eduardo's uncomplicated birth. According to *abuela* Elvira, Lorena had failed to bond with her second-born son, and as Diego had grown up his resemblance to his father had caused his mother to reject him even more.

His eyes were drawn to Rachel's belly and he felt a surge

of empathy with the child she carried within her. 'Don't you want our baby, Rachel?' he queried harshly.

He was doing it again—stirring her emotions with the words *'our baby'*. Rachel bit her lip as she thought back over the past few months when she had almost resented the child she had never expected to conceive. 'It's not that I don't want it,' she said shakily, 'but, more importantly, I want what is best for the baby.' She glanced around the dingy bedsit. 'I don't have the means to bring up a child, but there are hundreds of couples who are desperate for a baby, and who are in a better financial situation to give it a happy, secure upbringing with two parents who will love it.'

'Are you saying then that you do not think *we* can do all those things?'

Rachel gave Diego a scathing glance. 'There is no we, Diego. Until yesterday you didn't know I was pregnant, and I had no way of contacting you. If you hadn't shown up, you would never have known you had fathered a child.'

The idea that Rachel could have had his baby and handed it over to adoptive parents made Diego's blood run cold. He was startled by the feelings of protectiveness and possessiveness that swept through him, and by the realisation that he would love his child unconditionally.

'Tell me honestly,' he demanded harshly. 'If you were in a situation where you could bring up the child properly, would you want to keep it? Would you love it?'

It was so unexpected to hear cool, controlled Diego talk about love, in a voice deepened by emotion, that tears stung Rachel's eyes. 'Of course I would love it,' she whispered, images of a tiny dark-haired infant swirling in her mind. Did Diego believe she had contemplated putting her baby up for adoption lightly? 'Of course I would.'

'Then there is only one thing to be done.' For the first time in twenty-four hours, a feeling of calm settled over Diego— an acceptance of the inevitable and a realisation that there could only be one resolution to the situation. Since Eduardo's death, he had deliberately avoided relationships where his emotions might become involved, but he would not abandon his child, and he could not spend the rest of his life running away. 'You will marry me, Rachel, and we will bring our child up together in Argentina.'

Rachel's legs suddenly felt like jelly, although whether because of shock at Diego's outrageous statement or the effects of the flu virus, she did not know. Possibly both, she conceded as she sank weakly down onto the bed. A dozen responses whirled in her aching head, but one thought took precedence over all the others.

'My mother married my father because she was pregnant with me—and, trust me, it really didn't work. I have no intention of repeating my parents' mistakes,' she told him fiercely.

For a moment he made no reply, just stood watching her intently as if he was determined to read her mind. 'As a matter of fact, my mother and father married for the same reason,' he said coolly. 'I have no memories of my father—apparently he walked out when my twin brother and I were babies. But clearly a shotgun wedding didn't work for my parents, either.'

Rachel gave him a startled glance. It was the first time he had ever mentioned his family and she was annoyed with herself for wanting to hoard any small snippet of information about him. 'I didn't know you have a twin. Are you identical?' It seemed impossible that there was another man as dynamic and possessing the same powerful magnetism as Diego in the world.

'We were alike, but not identical,' he said abruptly.

'Were?' Rachel murmured hesitantly.

'My brother died ten years ago.'

Diego's tone warned Rachel not to pursue the subject, but she caught the flare of pain in his eyes and her heart contracted. To lose a twin must be devastating. She thought of her twin half-sisters from her mother's third marriage. Emma and

Kate were five now. They shared such a close bond that each seemed to know what the other twin was thinking, and when they spoke they frequently finished each other's sentences. She could not imagine how one of her sisters would function without the other, and she wondered how Diego had coped with his terrible loss.

During the month they had spent together she had believed him to be the wealthy, successful but emotionally shallow playboy he liked to portray. The passion they had shared had been electrifying, but she realised now that she hadn't known the real Diego Ortega at all.

'If a marriage of convenience didn't work for either of our parents, why suggest it when you know it's doomed to failure…?' she began, but he cut her off.

'What did you want more than anything when you were growing up, Rachel?'

'A horse,' she said tersely, wondering where the conversation was leading. She cast her mind back over her childhood and shrugged. 'Actually, what I wanted more than anything was to be my friend Clare—to live in a normal family with a mum and dad who weren't for ever screaming abuse at each other. Clare's parents liked each other, and I've always thought that that's how marriage should be—an equal partnership, friendship…'

'It seems that we share the same views on marriage,' Diego said quietly. 'As a child, I too wished that I had two parents who loved and cared for me.' Rather than a mother who despised him because he was a constant reminder of the man who had broken her heart. 'I think that for the sake of our child we could be friends, Rachel, and have the kind of marriage you described.

'We were friends once,' he reminded her when she stared at him in stunned silence. 'Until the day we went to Ascot, we had a good relationship.' They had shared a closeness that he had neither sought nor expected and, although he hated to admit it, he had missed her when she had abruptly ended their affair. 'I ended my friendship with Guy Chetwin, by the way. And threatened him with legal action if he ever insulted you again,' he added grimly.

Diego would be a dangerous adversary, Rachel thought with a shiver as she stared at his hard face. But she felt a little thrill of pleasure that he had defended her. It was true that they had shared friendship, as well as incredible sex while he had been at Hardwick, but for her it had been more than that. She had fallen in love with him. But when they had argued at Ascot he had bluntly told her that he had never planned on their affair leading to any kind of permanent relationship. It would be emotional suicide to marry a man who would never love her.

'Getting married is a mad idea,' she muttered. 'It would never work.' Her head was pounding worse than ever and every muscle in her body was aching with the effects of the flu virus. She wished Diego would go away and leave her alone, but he was looming over her, big and powerful and with a determined glint in his eyes that made her heart sink. He was difficult enough to fight at the best of times and right now she was in no fit state to do battle with him.

'So what do you suggest?' he demanded forcefully. 'You are carrying the heir to the Ortega fortune. I want our child to be born legitimately, and I am determined to take an active role in its life. Can you really deny the baby his or her birthright?'

Could she? What right did she have to deprive the baby of its father? And how could she think straight when her head was about to explode? 'I don't know what to do,' Rachel admitted weakly. She closed her eyes—as if by blotting Diego from view she could make him disappear. She had never expected him to reappear in her life, and she was even more stunned by his avowal that he wanted his child.

'It's not just a question of getting married,' she muttered. 'I'd have to move to the other side of the world to a strange country…'

'Argentina is not a strange country,' Diego assured her, his mouth curving into a sudden smile that made her heart turn over. 'It is a beautiful, vibrant country and I promise you will fall in love with it, *querida*.'

He was startled to see a tear trickle from beneath Rachel's lashes, and he felt a pang of guilt. She was clearly unwell, and he knew that in all fairness he should wait until she was feeling stronger before he demanded an answer to his proposal. But life wasn't always fair, and he had no compunction about seizing his opportunity. He wanted his child, and that meant he would have to persuade Rachel to marry him.

He dropped down onto the bed and tugged her into his arms, faintly surprised that she put up no resistance. This quiet, biddable Rachel would not be around for long. Once she had recovered from the virus that had caused her to look like death he was certain her usual feistiness would return, but for now she simply rested her head against his chest while he stroked his hand through her mane of long blonde hair.

He had forgotten how silky it was, and how soft her skin felt beneath his fingertips when he brushed a tear from her face. He liked her new rounded shape, and as he tightened his arms around her so that her full breasts were pressed against him he felt the slow burn of desire ignite inside him. *Dios!* She was heavy with child and burning up with a fever, yet he was more turned on than he had been for months. His desire for her was an unexpected complication—but perhaps not, he mused as he shifted position in an effort to ease the throb of his arousal. He had no great yearning to marry, but there was a child to consider, and at least he knew that he and Rachel were sexually compatible.

'Let me take care of you and the baby,' he murmured, brushing his lips over her hair.

His words struck a chord deep inside Rachel, and the feel of his strong arms around her evoked a desperate longing for him to protect her. If she was honest, she was scared witless about the future and she was tired of putting on a brave face and assuring herself and everyone that she would cope as a single mother. She did not want to do this on her own, and she did not want to give up her baby, she acknowledged, feeling a knife skewer her heart at the thought.

If she had been feeling herself she might have put up more of an argument against marrying Diego, but she felt physically and emotionally drained. He had offered to take care of her and right now those words, uttered in his deep, sensuous voice, drove her doubts to the back of her mind.

'When were you thinking of getting married?' she croaked, her hand straying to her stomach.

He placed his hand next to hers and she saw the faintly startled look in his eyes when he found that her bump was solid. 'I'll make the necessary arrangements immediately,' he said coolly. 'We don't have much time.'

CHAPTER NINE

THEY drove up to Diego's London apartment that day. Rachel slept for most of the journey and spent the following week in bed, so weakened by the virus that she did not even have the energy to argue with Diego when he brought meals to her room on a tray and stood over her until she had eaten enough to satisfy him.

She was dismayed by how little resistance she put up when he bossed her around, and how much she enjoyed being fussed over—even though she knew his concern was for the baby rather than her. She had been fiercely independent for so long that it was frightening to realise that she was turning into one of those pathetic women who meekly gave way to their husband on everything—and they weren't even married yet! But when Diego smiled at her she felt as though her insides were melting, and when he leaned over her bed to plump up her pillows she ached for him to lower his mouth to hers and kiss her until kissing was no longer enough for either of them and he traced his hands over her eager body.

But he never did. He was attentive and charming now that he had won the marriage argument, but nothing in his manner suggested that he found her sexually attractive.

It was hardly surprising, Rachel conceded three weeks later, on the morning of their wedding, when she donned the pale blue maternity dress and matching swing-coat which had cost a fortune from a top design house. The coat was cleverly cut to disguise the fact that she was heavily pregnant but she still felt like a ship in full sail, and there was nothing sexy about her big round football stomach, she decided ruefully.

Diego had arranged for Jemima Philips, the stylist who had helped Rachel choose an outfit for Ascot, to accompany her on a shopping trip for her trousseau. The irony of searching for a maternity bridal outfit six months after she had last been in London buying sexy underwear to seduce Diego was not lost on her. At least she had stuck to her guns and refused to buy a dress that was white, cream or overtly bridal, she mused. She was not a blushing bride, and Diego was far from a loving groom. They were marrying for purely practical reasons— although the doubts that Rachel had conveniently ignored while she had been ill were multiplying at a frantic rate now that she was better.

'We can be good parents to the baby without being married,' she had reasoned when he had informed her that they would be flying to Argentina immediately after their civil wedding. But the results of the DNA test which Diego had insisted on had proved beyond doubt that he was the baby's father, and he was utterly determined that his child would be born legitimately.

'So what do you suggest?' he demanded when she admitted that she was having second thoughts about becoming his wife. 'That I should set you up in an apartment in Buenos Aires— where you don't know a soul—so that I can visit my child on alternate weekends? Or were you thinking of remaining in England and sending our son or daughter over to Argentina for the school holidays? If that's the kind of life you want for our child then I'll fight for custody and bring the baby up in Argentina on my own.'

'You wouldn't win custody,' Rachel said faintly, shaken by the cold implacability in Diego's eyes. He had been so nice to her when she was ill, and she had been pathetically eager to grasp any sign that he might care for her a little, but this was the real Diego, hard and powerful and used to having his own way.

His smile held no warmth as he said, 'Losing isn't in my vocabulary, *querida*. I can afford the best lawyers, and the fact that you had considered putting the baby up for adoption would be a strong argument against allowing the child to remain with you.'

'But you know I only considered it because I felt the baby would have a better life with adoptive parents than I could give it,' she cried. 'I have only ever wanted what is best for the baby.'

'Then stop fighting with me,' Diego told her bluntly. 'It's not good for your blood pressure.'

The wedding took place at Westminster Register Office at eleven o'clock on a wet Friday morning, and was witnessed by Diego's chauffeur and the housekeeper from his London apartment. Rachel had turned down his offer to invite her family, explaining that her parents could not be in the same room together without old hostilities resurfacing.

It was a stark reminder of the pitfalls of a marriage of convenience. What would happen if in two or three years' time, she and Diego could not bear the sight of each other? She would never put her child through the misery of divorce and torn loyalties, she vowed fiercely. Somehow this marriage that had begun so inauspiciously had to work, and for the baby's sake, she would try her hardest to settle in a new country with a man who did not love her.

As they stood in the waiting room before their marriage ceremony Diego suddenly disappeared and returned moments later to hand her an exquisite bouquet of yellow roses. 'It is customary for a bride to have flowers on her wedding day,' he said quietly when Rachel could not hide her surprise.

Theirs was not a conventional marriage and she had not even thought about flowers, but for some reason Diego's unexpected gesture moved her deeply and she blinked hard to dispel the sudden rush of tears that filled her eyes.

'Thank you. They're beautiful,' she murmured huskily, remembering how he had given her yellow roses when he had visited her caravan after she had been thrown from her horse, and the passion that had flared between them when he had kissed her. She wondered if he remembered too, but his closed expression told her nothing and she felt sick with nerves when they stood before the registrar and made their vows. Diego looked impossibly handsome in a charcoal-grey suit, his dark hair brushing his shoulders, and she felt a sharp stab of longing for him to take her in his arms and kiss her as she longed to be kissed instead of brushing his cool lips over hers in a perfunctory gesture.

Immediately after the ceremony Diego assisted her into the waiting limousine for the journey to the airport. The same doctor who had performed the paternity tests on the baby had signed a special consent to allow Rachel to fly, even in her advanced stage of pregnancy. In truth, her heart had sunk at receiving the permission, the last hope for legitimately refusing to go along with Diego's plans removed.

'You won't be able to take your bouquet onto the plane,' he told her when she refused to leave it at the register office.

Rachel felt a fierce reluctance to part with her one memento of her wedding day, and while Diego was looking out of the window she quickly untied the yellow ribbon that secured the roses and slipped it into her handbag.

As the car joined the queue of Christmas getaway traffic into Heathrow, he turned back to her and handed her a small velvet box. 'Your wedding gift,' he murmured, wondering why the wariness in her eyes made him want to pull her into his arms and hold her close.

She was still pale, he noted. There had been a moment during the wedding ceremony when he had feared she would refuse to go through with it, and tension had churned in his gut. But after a few agonising seconds she had made her vows and now, for the first time in days, he could relax.

He had achieved what he wanted; his child would be born in Argentina and would bear the Ortega name. And he had a wife whom he desired more than any other woman, Diego acknowledged with a self-derisive smile. If someone had told him six months ago that he would spend night after sleepless night fantasising about making love to a woman in the later stages of pregnancy, he would have laughed. But it was no laughing matter. He wanted to lie next to Rachel and run his hands over her swollen stomach where his child was growing; he longed to cradle her breasts, which were no longer small but enticingly full, and he ached to gently part her pale thighs and position his body between them.

But something deep inside him told him it would be wrong to suggest that she shared his bed. She was no longer his mistress but the mother of his child, and he had a responsibility towards her that he'd never had for any other woman. Added to that, she was still recovering her strength from the flu virus, as well as coping with the demands of pregnancy and, although she tried to hide it, she was patently nervous about moving to a country she had never even visited before. The last thing she needed was a husband demanding his marital rights, and he would just have to control his urges and give her time to adjust to her new life.

'Open it,' he murmured when Rachel remained staring at the box as though she feared it might explode.

With fumbling fingers she flipped open the lid and caught her breath at the sight of an oval sapphire surrounded by diamonds which sparkled with fiery brilliance against the velvet surround.

'It's incredible,' she said faintly, because he was plainly waiting for her to say something. The ring was the most spectacular piece of jewellery she had ever seen and she couldn't imagine what it must have cost. But money was no object to

Diego and she did not kid herself that he had bought her a ring for sentimental reasons.

Her doubts were confirmed when he murmured, 'I know you should have had an engagement ring before the wedding, but it's a bespoke piece which I had made to match a necklace of the same design. We've been invited to numerous social functions in Buenos Aires over the Christmas period, and you'll need some jewellery.'

He lifted her hand and slid the ring next to her wedding band. It felt heavy and, although it fitted perfectly, it looked too big and cumbersome on her slender finger. It certainly wasn't something she would have worn when she had worked at the stables, but she was unlikely to be mucking out loose boxes any time soon, Rachel thought dismally.

She remembered how Diego had insisted on her wearing a designer outfit and an eye-catching diamond choker to Ascot. She had felt as though he had bought her—a feeling made worse when Guy Chetwin had accused her of being a gold-digger. Would Diego's friends in Argentina share the same view? she thought worriedly.

'How far is your ranch from Buenos Aires?' she asked curiously.

'The Estancia Elvira is about a hundred kilometres north of the city. It takes a little over an hour by road, but I usually commute by helicopter.'

'Commute?' Rachel frowned. 'But you live at the… *estancia*, don't you?'

'No, I prefer to live in town,' Diego said shortly. 'I have a penthouse apartment in the Puerto Madero district of Buenos Aires. There are fantastic views over the port and the city from the forty-second floor, and the shops and nightlife are excellent.'

Rachel's spirits dipped. She disliked heights, loathed shopping, and she didn't relish hitting the nightclubs at her advanced stage of pregnancy. But presumably Diego enjoyed an active social life in Buenos Aires. Would he expect her to accompany him on nights out, she wondered, or did he intend to visit nightclubs without the encumbrance of a heavily pregnant wife?

'But we will stay at the *estancia* sometimes, won't we?' she pressed. The only occasions during their stay in London that Diego hadn't seemed like a stranger was when they had discussed his polo pony breeding programme, and she had been looking forward to living on his ranch, close to the horses.

He gave a faint shrug. 'Perhaps I will take you after the baby is born, but for now it will be better to live in town, close to the amenities. The roads are good, but the *estancia* is still a long way from the hospital.' And it still held too many memories, Diego thought heavily. When he was at the stables he concentrated solely on the horses, but at the *hacienda* where he and Eduardo had spent their childhoods he was bombarded with scenes from the past, and he would swear he had sometimes heard his brother's voice echoing through the corridors. There were too many ghosts at the ranch house, and he did not need reminding of how he had failed Eduardo.

The flight to Argentina took fourteen hours, with a brief stopover at Sao Paolo airport in Brazil. As the plane began its descent over Buenos Aires, Rachel was shocked by the scale of the city and the hundreds of skyscrapers stretching for as far as she could see. It was a stark contrast to the small village in Gloucestershire where she had spent most of her life, and she felt a jolt of panic at the thought of trying to find her way around unfamiliar streets when she didn't speak a word of Spanish.

The heat and humidity when they walked out of the airport building to the waiting car was another shock after the cold winter they had left behind in England.

'The penthouse is fully air-conditioned,' Diego explained when she waved her hand in front of her hot face and asked if it was always this warm. 'The apartment block has a private pool, and there is a gymnasium if you want to get your figure back after the baby is born.'

Rachel stared down at her big stomach and wondered if it would ever go back to its pre-pregnancy flatness. Would Diego show an interest in her again if she worked out and regained her slender shape—or had his desire for her died completely? They had never discussed the physical aspect of their marriage, and as they'd spent their wedding night on the plane the question of sex hadn't come up. Would it tonight? she wondered, her heart rate quickening. Would Diego expect her to share his bed now that she was his wife?

She had her answer when they stepped out of the lift, a dizzying forty-two storeys from ground level, and Diego ushered her into his penthouse home. Jet lag and nervous tension had combined to make Rachel feel limp with tiredness and her eyes were huge in her pale face as she followed him from room to room, wondering how the cream velvet carpets and silk sofas would fare once the baby grew into an inquisitive, sticky-fingered toddler.

'You look exhausted,' Diego commented tersely, assuring himself that it was natural for him to feel concerned for Rachel, as well as for the baby. He scooped her into his arms, ignoring her yelp of surprise, and strode down the hall. 'I'll show you to your room and you can rest for a few hours. Tonight we'll eat at one of my usual restaurants and if you're up to it I'll give you a tour of the local area.'

Rachel nodded, her heart racing from the all too brief pleasure of being held against his chest. When he lowered her onto the pretty pink bedspread she wished he would stretch out next to her, but he quickly straightened up and moved away from the bed.

'We won't be able to eat out once the baby is here,' she murmured. When she had stayed at the cottage with him at Hardwick, Diego had frequently arranged for dinner to be delivered from a nearby restaurant, and it seemed that he still had an aversion to the kitchen.

'I realise that and I have already advertised for a cook. I suppose I will have to become more domesticated,' he said, sounding distinctly unenthusiastic at the prospect. Was he already regretting bringing her here? Rachel wondered, watching him prowl around her room like a caged tiger. There was something wild and primal about Diego and she could not imagine him settling down to a life of cosy domesticity. But he had insisted on marrying her, she reminded herself. And, for the baby's sake, they would both have to adjust and make the best of it.

To her amazement, adapting to her new life in Argentina did not prove as hard as Rachel had anticipated. Diego had withdrawn from his next polo tournament because it would have meant immediately flying to the Bahamas, and he gave her several guided tours of Buenos Aires, although he insisted on taking frequent breaks at street cafés so that she could rest.

'You'll find that Buenos Aires is a cosmopolitan city, with a strong European influence,' he explained as they strolled around the district of La Boca, where the unusual tin houses were painted in rainbow colours. 'The Portenos—as the citizens of Buenos Aires are called—are a multicultural people, and you will hear Italian and German spoken just as much as Spanish.'

It was a pity she did not speak any of those languages, Rachel mused. Diego had been shocked when she had admitted that she had never travelled outside England, and she felt ill-educated and unworldly when he revealed that he had visited practically every capital city in the world. Bustling, vibrant Buenos Aires was light years away from anything she'd ever experienced, but she enjoyed their trips to the famous Plaza de Mayo with its beautiful fountains, and the spectacular pink Presidential palace, and her heart had leapt when Diego linked his fingers through hers as they strolled through the old district of San Telmo, exploring the narrow streets lined with antique shops and artists' studios, pausing to watch dancers perform a breathtakingly sensual tango in one of the little courtyards.

Rachel was captivated by the raw energy of the city, but she was less enthusiastic when they went shopping. The Avenida Alvear housed many of the top designer establishments and Diego whisked her into Prada, Louis Vuitton and Versace, where she was fitted for several stunning but ludicrously expensive maternity evening gowns.

'I won't need maternity clothes in a few weeks,' she argued, praying it was true and that she wouldn't spend the rest of her life resembling a beach ball.

'I've already explained that we've been invited to various events over Christmas,' Diego replied. 'And tomorrow night one of my closest friends, Federico, and his wife Juana are throwing a party to celebrate our marriage.'

Rachel's mind flew to the one and only other social event she had attended with Diego. She had felt horribly out of place at Ascot, among his wealthy friends, and here in Argentina her inability to speak Spanish would surely be another barrier.

'You'll like Rico and Juana,' Diego assured her, feeling a curious tugging sensation on his heart at her dismayed expression. 'Their daughter Ana is two years old, and Juana has just announced that she is expecting another child.'

Federico Gonzalez and his wife lived in a large Spanish-style house in a leafy suburb of the city—and were as friendly and charming as Diego had promised. Juana was pretty and plump. 'I piled on *pounds* when I was expecting Ana,' she confided to Rachel, 'and now there's another baby on the way. But fortunately Rico says he likes me curvy.'

Rachel was grateful that Juana was so down-to-earth

because most of Diego's other friends were cultured socialites, members of the jet set whose wealth and sophistication
made her feel horribly gauche. They politely hid their curiosity
about her and took care to speak to her in English, but she
knew nothing about fine wines or opera, and even less about
politics, and found that she had little in common with them.

Among themselves the other guests chatted in Spanish, and
as Rachel listened to the babble of incomprehensible words
she felt increasingly isolated. She looked around for Diego
and saw him walking towards her.

'Where did you disappear to?' he murmured when he
reached her side.

'I went up to the nursery with Juana to meet little Ana. She's
the sweetest baby,' Rachel said, her face softening as she
thought of the cherubic toddler, who had still been wide
awake, playing with her nanny. It seemed hard to believe that
soon she would be holding her own baby. This time last year
she'd had no idea that Diego would storm into her life, but now
here she was, heavily pregnant and the wife of a man who had
only married her to claim his child.

'Not long now,' Diego said softly, watching the play of
emotions on her face. He could not take his eyes off Rachel
tonight. He had read in one of the many pregnancy and child-
birth books he'd been studying that pregnant women often
glowed, and he had wondered what that meant. Now he knew.

She had caught the sun while they had been walking
around the city and her face was lightly tanned, her cheeks
flushed a soft rose-pink that emphasised the dense blue of her
eyes. Her blonde hair was rich and lustrous, tumbling around
her shoulders, and the dress she had chosen for tonight—
layers of blue chiffon that skimmed her bump—was a perfect
foil for the sapphire and diamond necklace that matched her
engagement ring.

But her loveliness was more than a designer dress and jewellery, he mused. She was serene and slightly distant, as

though her thoughts were focused on the child she carried, and Diego found that he wanted to be included in that special, secret bond between mother and baby.

'No,' Rachel murmured, wondering if he was tired of her looking like an elephant and impatient for the baby to arrive. As if on cue, the baby kicked, the movement clearly visible beneath her dress. Diego looked startled.

'Was that…? Doesn't it hurt?'

'Not really, but the kicks are definitely getting stronger.'

Diego was staring at her stomach with an absorbed expression that, for some inexplicable reason, made Rachel want to cry.

'May I?' he asked huskily, moving his hand over her stomach.

Wordlessly, Rachel nodded. The warmth of his palm through her dress was enticing. It was so long since he had touched her body. Her heart began to thud and her breathing quickened. The baby kicked again. Did he or she recognise its father? she wondered mistily. She met Diego's gaze and her heart contracted at the emotion blazing in his amber eyes. Unquestionably, he would love his child. But what about her? a voice in her head demanded. Would she ever be anything to him other than the mother of his baby?

'He's obviously going to have a career as a footballer,' Diego murmured as the distinct shape of a tiny heel drummed against his hand.

'*She* might be a ballerina,' Rachel retorted.

He threw back his head and laughed. 'One thing's for sure, he or she is destined to be stubborn and argumentative—just like their mother.'

Rachel blushed but lifted her chin. 'I suppose you'd like me to be amenable and biddable and agree with everything you say,' she muttered crossly.

'I'd like to see the day you become amenable,' Diego choked, his eyes gleaming with amusement. He paused and then said quietly, 'I like you just the way you are, *querida*.'

Rachel did not know how to respond to that startling statement, but the warmth in Diego's gaze filled her with a tremulous hope that maybe they could work things out between them. She hesitated for a moment and then voiced the fear that had been gnawing at her all evening. 'Will we bring our child up to speak English or Spanish? Juana speaks to her daughter in Spanish… naturally…' She broke off, unable to explain how she'd felt when it had hit her that Diego would undoubtedly wish for his child's first language to be Spanish. It was bad enough that she could not chat to his friends, but the idea that she would be unable to communicate with her own child was terrible.

'I imagine we will bring him or her up to be bilingual,' Diego replied.

'That's fine for you, because you can speak both languages fluently.' Rachel bit her lip. 'You'll be able to chat away to our child in Spanish, but I'll be left out—and when we go to parents' evenings at school I won't know how he or she is progressing…' Her voice rose slightly. She was swamped by the very real fear that she would spend her life alienated from her environment and her baby, and tears flooded her eyes. 'Diego…I need to learn Spanish, but I was hopeless at languages at school. I failed French abysmally.'

Her vulnerability tore at Diego's insides. Unlike the many women he had met who could turn on the tears when it suited them, Rachel rarely cried. She gave the impression that she was strong and independent, but he suddenly appreciated how frightened she must have felt, moving to a new country with different customs, lifestyle and language.

'I will teach you Spanish, *querida*,' he promised gently. 'And with me as your tutor you will not fail.' He lifted his hand to her face and wiped away her tears. 'Every day we will spend an hour where I will show you the written language but, more importantly, we will talk in Spanish and you'll be surprised at how quickly you pick it up.'

He drew her into his arms and inhaled the delicate fragrance of her perfume. 'This is your first lesson. *Me siento muy orgulloso de mi hermosa esposa.* Do you want to know what that means?'

Rachel nodded, her eyes locked with his dark gaze and her heart beating too fast.

'It means—I am very proud of my beautiful wife.'

'Oh…' She did not know what to say, but suddenly words seemed unimportant as Diego lowered his head and brushed his mouth over hers in a butterfly caress that left her aching for more. She wrapped her arms around his waist, afraid that he intended to pull away, but instead he traced the shape of her lips with his tongue and then claimed her mouth once more in a slow, drugging kiss that stirred her soul.

'From now on you tell me immediately if something is troubling you,' he ordered when he eventually lifted his head and they both dragged oxygen into their lungs. 'I am your husband, Rachel, and it is my duty to care for you and protect you.'

His smile stole her breath, and she tried to ignore the little flutter of hurt that he regarded his role as her husband as a duty. It was unrealistic to hope he would fall in love with her as she loved him, she reminded herself. But they had been friends, as well as lovers, during their affair—and only a few moments ago he had told her that he liked her. That was a start, wasn't it?

Diego was shocked by how sweetly seductive it had felt to press his body against Rachel's soft curves. He had hardened the moment he had taken her into his arms, and the urge to lead her out into the dark garden where they would be alone and he could run his hands freely over her gorgeous pregnant shape was almost overwhelming. Calling on all his willpower, he eased away from her and stroked his finger lightly over her swollen mouth.

'I'll go and find us some drinks. Will you be all right on your own for a few minutes?' He needed to bring his raging hormones under control.

'Of course.' Rachel watched him stride across the room,

her heart sinking when she noted the many admiring glances he drew from the female guests. His stunning looks made him a magnet for the opposite sex but, to give him credit, he seemed unaware of the interest he aroused.

A waiter appeared at her side, offering a selection of sweet pastries, and she could not resist the sugar-covered *churros*, which were similar to small English doughnuts, or the little layered cakes filled with chocolate that the waiter told her were called *alfajores*.

'I'm going to be the size of a house if I keep eating these,' she said guiltily to Juana, who had just joined her.

Juana gave a faint smile but her eyes were troubled. 'Rachel… Lorena Ortega has arrived and she's asked to meet you.' Juana grimaced. 'Lorena is Diego's mother. I had to invite her to the party, of course, but she told me she wasn't coming. I can't believe she's turned up.' Juana looked even more awkward. 'I expect you know that Diego and his mother don't get on. They never did, not even when Diego was a child, and of course after the accident…well…' Juana broke off. 'It's no secret that Lorena adored Eduardo and rejected Diego. The thing is, she's asked to see you alone. But you don't have to. I wanted to warn Diego she's here, but Federico has dragged him off to admire his new toy—and, knowing my husband and cars, they could be hours.'

Rachel shrugged. 'I'm quite happy to meet Diego's mother.' If she was honest, she was intensely curious to meet Lorena Ortega because Diego had never spoken about her.

She followed Juana along the hall and into what she guessed was Federico's study.

'Lorena, this is Rachel,' Juana said as she ushered Rachel into the room.

Diego's mother must have been a beauty in her youth, and even now she was older she had retained her classically sculpted features and enviably slim figure. But her face was lined, her mouth set in a permanent droop of dissatisfaction and her dark eyes were dulled. She was also drunk, Rachel realised as she stepped into the room and waited while Lorena drained a glass of spirits and set the glass down with an unsteady hand.

'So you're Diego's little wife.' Her eyes roamed over Rachel and she gave a mirthless laugh. 'And you're pregnant. Well, I'm surprised it hasn't happened before now. My son's list of mistresses is legendary.'

She waved her hand imperiously, indicating that Rachel should sit down, and refilled her glass with brandy. 'Would you like a drink?'

'No, thank you.' Rachel instinctively moved her hand to her stomach.

Lorena's eyes narrowed. 'You're just a child—a child who, no doubt, was seduced by a man who should have known better.'

Rachel shook her head. 'That's not true,' she said firmly. 'Diego didn't seduce me. I knew what I was doing.'

Lorena shrugged. 'Your loyalty is touching, but I fear it won't be repaid. I was your age when I met Diego's father. I was young, naïve, hopelessly in love. But Ricardo was a playboy and an opportunist, and he didn't want me—he wanted my money. My father saw him for what he was immediately, but by then it was too late. I was pregnant, and blinded by love for Ricardo. I was grateful when he offered to marry me.

'I didn't know about his other women, not at first,' Lorena spat, seemingly unaware of Rachel's shocked silence in the face of her venomous diatribe. 'But as the months and my pregnancy progressed and I became grossly huge, Ricardo no longer bothered to keep the reason for his frequent trips to Buenos Aires a secret.

'I have always thought that if there had only been one child, if there had only been Eduardo, I would have retained Ricardo's interest,' she confided to Rachel, an unnerving wildness in her eyes. 'But what man would want to make love to a woman whose body is swollen and ugly? I did not have one baby, I had two, and giving birth to Diego nearly killed me.'

'But you can't blame Diego for that, or for your husband's infidelity,' Rachel said in a startled voice. 'How could anyone blame a baby for anything?' She bit her lip, remembering how in the weeks after she had learned that she was pregnant she had almost resented the child she had conceived by accident. She had blamed the baby for the fact that she could no longer ride or work at the stables, and for having to give up Piran. Fortunately she had come to her senses, but it was clear that Lorena Ortega's resentment of her son had begun before he had even drawn breath.

Lorena lifted her glass to her lips and took another long swig of brandy. 'If there had only been Eduardo…' she muttered, her voice slurring. She suddenly looked up and stared at Rachel with glazed eyes. 'Diego is a man like his father, mark my words. I believe there is an English expression—don't expect a leopard to change its spots? Diego has never remained faithful to one woman for long, and you're a fool if you think he'll start now.

'Diego was always wild and reckless,' Lorena continued morosely, 'while Eduardo was the finest son a mother could wish for. But now Eduardo is dead—,' her voice broke and she drained the brandy in another gulp '—and it's Diego's fault. Diego sent him to his death…'

'What do you mean…?' Rachel's heart was beating so fast she could barely breathe. She gasped, frantically trying to snatch air into her lungs, and when she heard a sound from behind her she jerked her head around.

Diego walked into the room. '*Hola, madre.*' His eyes swung suspiciously from Lorena Ortega, and the half empty bottle of brandy in front of her, to Rachel's pale face and he grimaced. 'I see you have been celebrating my marriage to Rachel. Is it too much to hope that you've been drinking to my good health?' he drawled sarcastically.

'Perhaps I have been commiserating with your wife on her choice of husband,' Lorena snapped.

'And no doubt warning her that I am a serial womaniser like my father was?'

'Well, that's the truth, isn't it, Diego?' Lorena glared at her son, and Rachel was shocked by the bitterness in the older woman's eyes. 'You and Ricardo were from the same mould. He even died in the arms of one of his harlots. I always knew cocaine would kill him.'

Diego strolled across the room and slid his arm around Rachel's waist, drawing her against him. She made no resistance, glad of his support, his strength and air of calm in contrast to his mother's emotional intensity.

'I'm taking Rachel home now,' he said quietly. 'It's been a long evening and I'm sure she must be tired.'

Rachel was so shocked by Lorena's startling accusation that Diego had somehow been involved in his twin's death that she said nothing and simply allowed him to steer her across the room. He halted in the doorway and glanced back at his mother. 'My child is your grandchild, *madre*. Do you not think you should try to forget the past and be a part of the baby's life?'

Lorena gave a harsh laugh. 'I will never forget,' she said viciously. She threw Diego a look of such loathing that Rachel gasped. 'Eduardo will never marry or have a child.' Hysteria edged into her voice. 'Everything was snatched away from him…'

The colour drained from Diego's face and Rachel was shaken by the flare of agony in his eyes. But he quickly masked his expression and nodded to his mother. '*Adios, madre*,' he murmured quietly, before he swept Rachel out of the room.

CHAPTER TEN

ON THE drive back to the penthouse Rachel could not face talking so she closed her eyes and pretended to be asleep. But she could not dismiss the image of Lorena Ortega throwing brandy down her throat and staring at Rachel with her wild eyes—and, worse than that, the look on Diego's face when Lorena had spoken of his twin brother, Eduardo. It was clear Lorena believed that Diego was somehow to blame for Eduardo's death. But when Rachel peeped through her lashes at Diego's grim face she dared not ask him for an explanation.

But whatever dark thoughts had been troubling him on the journey across town, he seemed to have dismissed them when they arrived back at the apartment.

'I knew you would like Juana,' he commented as he crossed to the bar in the lounge. Rachel knew he hadn't drunk alcohol all evening, and it was understandable that he would want a nightcap, but as he half filled a glass with brandy she was reminded vividly of his mother, and she could not restrain a shiver.

'Would you like a drink? I'll make you some tea.' He gave her the confident smile of a man who was no longer a stranger to the kitchen, and who had now mastered the intricacies of the teapot to make her tea first thing in the morning and every evening.

'No, thank you. I'm going straight to bed,' Rachel replied dully.

Diego frowned, noting how stiffly she held herself. She had seemed relaxed in the car and he'd assumed that meeting his mother hadn't bothered her as much as he had feared it might. Clearly he had been wrong.

'What's the matter, Rachel? Although I don't really need to ask,' he said grimly. 'Perhaps I should rephrase the question, and ask what my mother said to you.'

Rachel bit her lip, hearing again Lorena Ortega's cry that Diego had sent his brother to his death. It couldn't be true—could it? It had just been the drunken ramblings of an embittered woman. But why did Lorena hate her surviving son so much? She did not have the nerve to come straight out and ask Diego how Eduardo had died, and instead she dwelled on the other things his mother had said, in particular her assertion that Diego was a womaniser as his father had been.

'She said that your list of mistresses is legendary—and that you will never remain faithful to one woman,' she mumbled.

Diego's brows winged upwards and he gave her an arrogant stare. 'And of course you believed her—even though you had never met her before and it was obvious she'd had too much to drink? Thank you for your faith in me, *querida*,' he said icily.

It was impossible to believe she had hurt him, Rachel thought shakily—not when he was staring down his nose at her as if she were something unpleasant on the bottom of his shoe. She wanted to assure him that no, she hadn't believed a word his mother had said, but she could not forget the newspaper photo of him surrounded by gorgeous glamour models at the US open polo tournament, or the boldly flirtatious glances some of the women at the party had sent his way tonight.

'Have you had other lovers since me?' she burst out.

'I don't think that's any of your business.' His expression was glacial. 'You walked out on me, remember?' Nothing on earth would induce Diego to admit that he had felt gutted when she had abruptly ended their relationship.

His arrogance fuelled Rachel's temper. She had a sudden flashback to when she had been eight years old and she had watched her mother sobbing uncontrollably because she had discovered that Rachel's father was having an affair with his secretary. She wasn't prepared to live her life like that, always looking over her shoulder and wondering…

'I don't care how many women you slept with before we were married,' she told Diego fiercely. 'But now I am your wife, and if you think I will turn a blind eye to your extra-marital activities, think again.'

Diego surveyed her with an air of mocking amusement which did not disguise his anger. 'Perhaps I should remind you that you are hardly in the position to impose stipulations or make demands regarding our marriage,' he drawled. 'I married you for my child, and I will retain custody of the child should I ever decide to end our marriage.

'But I can see no reason why it should come to that,' he murmured in a marginally softer tone when Rachel paled. 'We both want to be good parents and give our child the stability that was missing from our own childhoods.' He reached out and ran his fingers through her hair, his brows lifting arrogantly when she tensed. 'Despite the impression my mother has given you that I am a lecherous playboy like my father, I give you my word that I am prepared to be a loyal and faithful husband.' His other hand snaked around her waist and he jerked her up against his chest, his eyes no longer icy, but blazing with a sensual intent that made Rachel catch her breath.

'I have been patient, *querida*, waiting for you to regain your strength after your illness, and giving you time to settle here in Argentina. But now it is time to make this marriage real, so that you can be in no doubt about my intention to please my wife in all the ways I know she likes best.'

'Diego…' Embarrassed colour scorched Rachel's cheeks

as she remembered her unabashed enjoyment of the many and varied ways he had made love to her during their affair. But her startled protest was muffled beneath his mouth as he lowered his head and claimed her lips in a devastating assault that obliterated her fear that his desire for her had died.

It had been months since he had kissed her properly, and so much had happened since then. She had learned that she was carrying his child—and he had been so angry when she'd told him, which in turn had fuelled her resentment and mistrust of him. But right now none of that seemed to matter. Her body had been denied him for so long, and it paid no heed to the warning voice in her head which taunted that sexual desire was not love—not for him, anyway. For Rachel it was inextricably linked—and that left her wide-open to being hurt.

Frantically she firmed her lips against the fierce thrust of his tongue, but Diego changed tactics and, instead of trying to force her lips apart, he began to tease her with soft, beguiling kisses, tasting her and sipping her so that her resistance slowly melted away. Her arms crept around him. He was so strong and powerful and she felt safe with him, and yet at the same time she knew she was in mortal danger of succumbing to his potent masculinity.

He trailed his lips over her cheek and down her throat to the pulse jerking wildly at its base. Every nerve-ending on Rachel's body sprang into urgent life and she gasped when he lowered his head to the deep valley between her breasts.

'I love what pregnancy has done to your body,' he murmured huskily, his breath feathering her skin. He closed his fingers possessively around one full breast, and Rachel felt her nipples swell and harden. 'You are more beautiful than ever, *querida*.'

Rachel laid her hands on his chest and felt the heat of his body through his shirt, and her senses swam as she caught the scent of his aftershave mingled with the subtle drift of male pheromones. Whatever had happened in his past, he was with her now and had vowed to be faithful to her. He did not love her, but he wanted to make love to her—and she could no longer deny her need for him, she acknowledged, sighing her pleasure when he captured her mouth once again.

She could not fight the insidious warmth spreading through her veins, the heaviness of her breasts and the dragging ache between her legs. Slowly she opened her mouth to him and heard his low groan as he slid his tongue deep into her moist warmth and explored her until she was trembling. It seemed the most natural thing in the world for him to sweep her up into his arms and stride down the hall to the master bedroom, and when he laid her on the rich burgundy silk bedspread she threaded her fingers through his long, dark hair and tugged him down on top of her.

He wanted her, and nothing else seemed important— because she wanted him too, her desperation to feel his satiny skin beneath her fingertips so great that she tore open his shirt with feverish haste and skimmed her palms over the bunched muscles of his abdomen.

'Slowly,' he bade her huskily, amusement at her eagerness mingling with a feral hunger he had never experienced with any other woman. 'We must be careful of the little one.'

But Rachel did not want to be careful. The baby was safely cocooned inside her, and she was burning up with need. She shifted obligingly onto her side so that Diego could unzip her dress, her breath coming in shallow gasps when he drew the material down to expose her sheer black lace bra.

'*Bella*,' he growled, dull colour flaring along his magnificent cheekbones as he stared down at her proudly erect nipples straining against the lace. He swiftly unfastened her bra and groaned his satisfaction when he cupped her naked breasts in his hands and felt their plump softness. 'It has been a long time since we were together, and I want you very badly,' he warned her.

Rachel wanted to tell him that her hunger was as urgent as his, but the words were trapped in her throat when he bent his dark head to her breast and took one rosy crest into his mouth, the sensations he evoked as he sucked making her twist her hips in a blatant invitation. She had relived him making love to her every night since they had parted, but her dreams had been no substitute for the feel of his hands and mouth sliding over her body. Her breasts were so acutely sensitive that when he transferred his mouth to her other nipple and teased the swollen peak with his tongue she cried out and anchored her fingers in his silky hair to hold him to this task of pleasuring her.

Heat flooded between her thighs and she was desperate for him to touch her there, but reality briefly impinged when he began to tug her dress over her hips.

'Leave it on,' she implored him, her face flaming. 'I look like a whale.'

'No, you don't. You are exquisite,' Diego said deeply as he allowed her dress to float to the floor and ran his hand possessively over the hard swell of her stomach. '*Dios*, Rachel, you carry my child within you, and you will never look lovelier than you do now.'

He kissed her mouth, and she sensed tenderness, as well as passion. The sensual sweep of his tongue dismissed the last lingering doubts, and she lifted her hips so that he could slide her knickers down her legs, sighing her pleasure when he gently parted her and probed delicately between the slick wet folds of her womanhood.

'Please, Diego—now,' she whispered, and the undisguised need in her voice shattered his restraint so that he jumped up and stripped out of his clothes before stretching out on the bed beside her.

The sight of his arousal still had the power to steal her breath. He was a magnificent bronzed demi-god, and Rachel gave a shiver of anticipation as she ran her hands over the dark whorls of hair that covered his chest, and followed the path over his flat stomach and lower, to where his throbbing erection was pushing impatiently against her belly.

How were they going to do this? she wondered, her heart sinking as she stared down at her stomach.

Diego noted her faint frown and smiled, his amber eyes gleaming. 'Like this,' he murmured as he helped her move to the edge of the bed so that her feet rested on the floor. He stood up, nudged her thighs apart and positioned himself between them, slid his hands beneath her bottom and, as he lifted her, he eased forwards and carefully entered her. He filled her so deeply that Rachel gave a little sob of pleasure, but he misunderstood and immediately stilled.

'Am I hurting you?'

'Only if you stop. I'm not breakable, I'm strong and fit and I want you to make love to me properly,' she told him, clutching his shoulders and urging him to thrust deeper still. 'Please, Diego, don't stop…don't stop.'

The sensation of having him move inside her was so exquisite that she wanted it to never ever end. He drove into her again, a little faster, a little harder, setting a rhythm that made her blood thunder through her veins as the nagging ache deep in her pelvis grew and grew. The pleasure was intolerable, it couldn't last, and suddenly she was there on the edge of ecstasy, and the spasms that began as tiny ripples deep inside her radiated out in an explosion of sensation that made her cry out as she shuddered with the intensity of her climax.

Only then, when he had taken her to the heights, did Diego's control falter. She was so tight and hot, and so generous, lifting her hips to meet the thrust of his. He was afraid of hurting her, but she was urging him on and he gripped her buttocks and drove into her one last time, felt the exquisite spasms of her vaginal muscles squeeze him and with a groan his control shattered and he pumped his seed into her.

For a few moments he rested his weight on her, his breathing ragged and his heart-rate gradually slowing. But he was aware that this must be uncomfortable for her and he drew her back up the bed, curling his arm around her as she laid her head on his chest.

She felt as though she had come home, Rachel thought dreamily. The sound of Diego's steady heartbeat beneath her ear was wonderfully familiar, and in the golden afterglow of sex she felt the same sense of closeness to him that she had loved during their affair. She loved him, and she finally accepted that there was no point in trying to fight her feelings for him. And, as she lay in his arms and felt him stroke her hair, she felt a wild sense of hope that he might care for her a little.

'How many women have you slept with since me?' she whispered, hating herself for sounding so needy, but needing to know.

He stiffened, and in the taut silence Rachel was sure he could hear the overloud thud of her heart. Slowly he turned his head on the pillow and met her gaze, a curious expression in his eyes that she could not define.

'None,' he grated, his mouth twisting into a self-derisive grimace. 'Dammit, Rachel. Sex with you was always explosive—as I've just proved,' he drawled. 'I don't mind admitting that you turn me on more than any other woman.

'Happy now?' he asked dryly when she could not hold back her smile.

Oh, yes! Happier than she'd believed possible. The fact that Diego hadn't made love to half a dozen beautiful models while they had been apart did not mean that he actually felt anything for her, she reminded herself. But at least she could banish the jealous demon from her head. There was only one other thing that was bothering her. She felt reluctant to bring up the subject of his brother, but she could not forget Lorena Ortega's accusation—and there was probably a simple explanation.

Diego watched the play of emotions on her face and wondered if she was aware that he could read every nuance. 'What is it, *querida*?'

'How did Eduardo die?'

'*Dios*, what made you ask that?' His reaction was instant and savage, his face hardening as he jerked away from her.

'I'm sorry, I was just curious,' Rachel stammered, wishing she had kept quiet as the harmony between them was shattered. 'It was just something your mother said…' She bit her lip and shrank back on the pillows as Diego leaned over her and pierced her with an icy stare that made her blood run cold.

'What did my mother say?' he demanded in a dangerously soft tone.

'She said that Eduardo's death was…was your fault. But I know that can't be true,' she whispered, her heart thudding painfully beneath her ribs when Diego did not immediately refute Lorena's allegation.

'But it is true, Rachel,' he said quietly, his voice no longer full of anger, but flat and lifeless. 'I was responsible for Eduardo's death. Not deliberately,' he continued, his gut clenching when he saw the flare of horror in her eyes. 'Eduardo was my twin; we were like two halves of a whole, and when he died…' Diego broke off, reliving the pain that had been almost unendurable when he had dragged Eduardo's lifeless body from the river. 'When he died, I wished I had died too,' he admitted rawly. 'But I did not die, and I have had to live with the knowledge that because of my hot temper, my wildness and irresponsibility which—as my mother constantly reminded me throughout my youth—were traits I inherited from my father, I caused the death of the person I loved most in this world.'

He would carry his guilt to the grave, Diego acknowledged silently, as he jumped up from the bed and dragged his clothes on. It ate away at him and tainted everything he did, hovering like a spectre over every moment of happiness and reminding him that he had no right to be happy when, because of him, Eduardo had been robbed of his life. Eduardo would never hold his wife in his arms and run his hands over her stomach that was swollen with his child. He would never experience the excitement of being a father, or look at his wife across a crowded room and feel a surge of pride that she was his woman and his alone.

Rachel's eyes were huge in her pale face, but her expression of curiosity had been replaced by one of compassion that tore at Diego's insides. He did not want compassion, did not deserve it. What right did he have to lie next to her in the blissful aftermath of making love, and feel a contentment he had never known before?

Suddenly he could not bear to be near her. She was so beautiful with her golden hair tumbling around her shoulders and her creamy breasts pouting at him invitingly, causing the familiar ache in his groin. He did not deserve her when Eduardo had nothing. And he would not give in to the temptation to confide in her that, far from being the hard, emotionless man he portrayed, he was a bloody mess. It was better to keep her at a distance and deal with his pain alone. Better to strengthen the barriers he had erected against the warmth of her smile.

'Where are you going?'

He had reached the door, but turned back at the tremulous sound of her voice. 'I'm leaving for a polo tournament in South Africa early in the morning. I don't want to disturb you, so I'll sleep in the spare room.'

'South Africa! Why didn't you tell me before now?' Rachel asked shakily. It was crazy, but she couldn't help thinking that Diego was running away from her.

He shrugged, refusing to admit that up until five minutes ago he had decided to pull out of the competition so that he could stay with her. 'You know I play all over the world. I'm afraid you'll have to get used to me disappearing at short notice.'

'But how long will you be gone? We have things to discuss,' she said desperately. 'Your brother...'

'What happened with Eduardo does not concern you,' Diego told her grimly. 'The only thing you need to think about is the baby. I will be away for less than a week, but I have arranged for Juana Gonzalez to come to the apartment to give you Spanish lessons. What with that and your antenatal classes, you will be too busy to miss me, *querida*,' he taunted.

Rachel flushed. Did he know that she would be counting the minutes until he returned? she wondered in an agony of embarrassment. And, if so, did he also guess that she was utterly besotted with him?

She sat up and pushed her hair over her shoulder, feeling a minute sense of triumph when his eyes lingered on her breasts and dull colour flared along his cheekbones. 'I'm sure I won't give you a second's thought,' she said coolly. 'Have a good trip.'

Diego came home from South Africa on Christmas Eve. He greeted Rachel with cool politeness and she went to bed alone soon after he arrived and wept silently into her pillow, wishing she could recapture the closeness they had briefly shared the night he had made love to her.

The following morning she was taken aback to find a pile of gifts beneath the Christmas tree, and she stiffly thanked him when she unwrapped a breathtaking pearl and diamond necklace and matching earrings, a solid white gold bracelet and a platinum ring set with an emerald the size of a rock. The jewellery must have cost a fortune, but she could not tell him that what she really wanted was the most priceless gift of all and the one thing, it seemed, he would never give—his love.

They spent Christmas Day with Federico and Juana, and in the following days attended numerous lavish parties thrown by Diego's many wealthy friends. Rachel grew used to being the focus of interest—it seemed that everyone was curious about the woman who had tamed Diego. Little did his friends know that once they returned to his apartment Diego invariably disappeared into his study, making no attempt to disguise the fact that he was avoiding her, Rachel thought bitterly, or that that they slept in different beds.

Once the festive period was over he settled into a routine of leaving home at dawn and travelling by helicopter to his ranch to the north of Buenos Aires. Rachel filled the long days while he was away chatting to Juana, who visited regularly or invited Rachel back to her home. She attended antenatal appointments and birthing classes and shopped in earnest for baby clothes and nursery equipment, amazed by the amount of paraphernalia required for one small baby.

But the heat and humidity of the city left her exhausted. She was thirty-six weeks pregnant and was convinced that if her stomach grew any bigger it would explode. Perhaps Diego spent all his time at the Estancia Elvira to avoid seeing her waddling around the apartment, she thought dismally. He had said that he found her pregnant shape beautiful, but she certainly did not feel beautiful, she felt huge and clumsy and horribly hormonal, which at least explained her tendency to burst into tears when no one was around to see.

It was understandable that she felt homesick, she thought one morning when she stepped out of the air-conditioned apartment onto the balcony and felt as though she had walked into a furnace. But in reality she hadn't had a proper home in England for years apart from her dilapidated old caravan. She wasn't so much homesick as horse-sick—which was ridiculous when she was married to a man who owned one of the largest polo pony stud farms in Argentina. She longed to visit the *estancia* and see the horses but, although she had asked Diego several times when he would take her, he had always made some excuse.

But Diego had said that the *estancia* was not much more than an hour's journey by road, she brooded as she stared out over the endless expanse of skyscrapers that stretched up to the sky like concrete giants, their hundreds of windows winking in the brilliant sunlight. If she left now she should arrive at the Estancia Elvira by late morning. Filled with a sudden restless excitement she ignored the niggling backache that had woken her in the early hours, threw a few basic necessities into a bag and put a call through to the chauffeur, Arturo.

Diego had spent the morning in the paddock, working with one of the *gauchos* to introduce a couple of four-year-old colts to the ball and mallet which were used in polo. But now the midday sun was at its hottest and it was time to give the ponies a break.

'The chestnut mare is showing particular promise,' he spoke to the *gaucho* in Spanish as they rode the horses back to the stable block.

Carlos nodded. 'Another good horse from the Estancia Elvira, huh, boss?' He paused and stared curiously along the dirt track at the figure some way in the distance. 'Boss…I think we've got a visitor.'

'There are no appointments today.' Diego broke off as he followed the *gaucho's* gaze, and then he swore savagely. '*Santa madre!* That woman would test the patience of a saint!' he growled before he urged his horse into a gallop and thundered along the track.

'What the *blazes* are you doing here?' he demanded when he halted in front of Rachel. She looked achingly lovely in a yellow sundress that left her slim shoulders bare and softly skimmed her rounded stomach. Her hair was caught up in a ponytail, secured with the yellow ribbon she always wore, but stray tendrils had escaped and curled around her face and Diego could not prevent his eyes from focusing on her soft pink mouth. 'You look like a buttercup,' he muttered, staring at her dress.

'More like a butter-pat,' she replied with a rueful glance at her sizeable bump.

'You should have stayed in town. The baby…'

'The baby isn't due for another month,' Rachel said serenely. In the past weeks Diego's preoccupation with the baby's well-being had driven her mad. She was sure he would wrap her in cotton wool and forbid her from leaving her bed if he had the chance, no matter that her obstetrician had assured them the baby's heartbeat was strong and Rachel's pregnancy was progressing normally.

She looked up at him, astride his horse. His dark hair brushed his shoulders and his hard-boned face was so beautiful that her heart turned over. 'It's so hot in the city, and I wanted to breathe fresh air and feel a breeze on my face. It's beautiful here,' she murmured, lifting her arms wide to encompass the view of two thousand acres of prime grassland, the horses grazing in the distance and the sprawling white-walled *hacienda* which was further up the track, surrounded by blue-flowered jacaranda trees.

'The sun is hot here too,' Diego growled impatiently, 'and I see you failed to have the good sense to wear a hat. You'd better get up to the house. The housekeeper, Beatriz, will be pleased to see you,' he said in a tone which clearly implied that he was not.

'I've already met her,' Rachel told him. 'When I first arrived, one of your ranch-hands showed me around the stables and then took me to the house. But Beatriz isn't there now. She told me she was going to visit her sister who lives on another farm.'

Diego nodded. 'I'd forgotten. She goes every week.' He looked up the track towards the *hacienda*. 'I need to take the horse back to the stables. Will you be all right to walk to the house—I'll meet you there as soon as I can?'

'Of course I'll be all right,' Rachel assured him firmly. She certainly was not going to mention that her backache was now acutely painful, she thought as she walked slowly up to the house. She had probably slept awkwardly and pulled a muscle, but she had to admit that she would be glad to sit down in the cool shade of the veranda that ran right around the *hacienda*.

At least Diego had not immediately demanded that she

should return to the city. The chasm that had opened between them when she had asked him about his brother's death was growing wider each day, and she knew she had to try and make him talk to her. She just prayed that here at his childhood home she would be able to reach him, and that one day soon he would smile at her again instead of treating her with a cool indifference that broke her heart.

CHAPTER ELEVEN

THERE was no sign of Rachel when Diego walked into the *hacienda*. He strode down the hall, his boots echoing on the terracotta stone floors as he searched the various big airy rooms on the ground floor. Little had changed over the years. The house seemed to be trapped in a time-warp, he brooded when he reached the kitchen and stared at the copper cooking pots hanging on the wall and the huge wooden table that Beatriz still scrubbed every day.

How many times had he and Eduardo sat at that table, eating *empanadas*—delicious meat-filled pasties—and watching Beatriz prepare the evening meal? He remembered how the cook used to give them a big bowl of peas to shell, and Eduardo had carefully prised open the pods while he had fired his peas at Beatriz until she had waved her wooden spoon at him and told him he was the devil's child.

Beatriz had been joking, but he was sure his mother and grandfather had truly believed he was one of Satan's offspring, he thought grimly. He had understood from an early age that his startling resemblance to his father had provoked his mother's hatred of him, but he hadn't cared. He'd had Eduardo and that was all that mattered...

Diego turned abruptly and strode out of the kitchen, taking the stairs to the second floor two at a time. He did not want to be here. He wanted to find Rachel and take her back to the

city, where the ghosts were still in his head but he was not surrounded by visual reminders of the past.

'Rachel…' he called impatiently.

'I'm in here.'

He followed the sound of her voice and halted in the
doorway of the bedroom directly across the hall from the
master bedroom.

'What are you doing?' he demanded, frowning at the sight
of her taking clothes out of a small suitcase and stowing them
in a drawer.

'Unpacking,' she replied brightly. 'I brought enough things
with me so that we could stay for a few days. Beatriz said that
you keep spare clothes here, and it seems silly to rush back
to town.' She did not add that she had planned to put her
things in Diego's room, hoping he would realise that she
wanted to share his bed, but that her nerve had failed her at
the last minute. From the deep frown furrowing his brow, her
decision had probably been unwise, she thought with a
sinking heart.

'Silly or not, that's what we're doing,' Diego said harshly. 'I
have no wish to stay here, and you are a few weeks away from
giving birth and need to be close to the hospital. You'd better
repack while I tell Arturo to bring the car down to the house.'

'You can't. I sent him back to town,' Rachel murmured,
steeling herself for Diego's angry response when his eyes
glittered dangerously. 'Diego…we can't carry on like this,' she
said shakily.

His brows rose. 'Like what?'

She quailed beneath his haughty stare, but forced herself
to go on. 'You…so cold…and distant.' How would he feel if
he knew she cried herself to sleep every night? 'I don't understand what happened in your past, but while it hangs over us
we can't begin to have a future. I thought we were friends,'
she whispered when he said nothing. 'In a few weeks our baby
will be born—the baby we vowed to give the happy childhood

that neither of us had. But how can we, Diego, when there is this terrible silence between us?'

Tears clung to her lashes, and the sight of them tore at Diego's insides. Rachel was right; they could not carry on avoiding his past. He hated the silence that hovered between them like a poisonous gas cloud, and he missed her laughter and her cheerful chatter, but more than anything he was swamped with a loneliness that felt like a knife in his ribs when he lay in bed every night and wished that she was curled up next to him, all warm and soft and so sexy that he ached for her.

Her cornflower-blue eyes were fixed on him, waiting. But he had never spoken about Eduardo's death to anyone and he could not face her as he revealed the guilt he had carried for ten long years. He swung away from her to stare unseeingly across the grasslands that surrounded the *hacienda*.

'I don't remember a time when my mother ever loved me,' he said harshly. 'She adored Eduardo but, as I grew older and my physical resemblance to my father became more marked, she seemed to hate me more. She had loved my father, you see, but his infidelity broke her heart and left her deeply bitter.

'My grandfather, Alonso, had always thought that my father had married Lorena for money. After their bitter divorce he persuaded her to revert back to her maiden name, and she also changed my and Eduardo's name to Ortega. But although I carried the family name, my grandfather—like my mother— believed that my resemblance to my father was more than just skin deep,' Diego continued bleakly. 'He made no secret that he intended to make Eduardo the sole heir to the Estancia Elvira.'

'That must have been hard,' Rachel said quietly. 'It would be understandable if you had been jealous of Eduardo.'

Diego shook his head. 'I was never jealous of him. He was my twin, and he was as much a part of me as one of my limbs. We spent all our time together, and shared everything. I didn't care what anyone else thought about me and, to be honest, Lorena and Alonso's dislike of me upset Eduardo more than it did me.

'But I rowed frequently with my grandfather. No matter what I did, and how hard I tried to please him and my mother, in their eyes I was a feckless playboy like my father.' Diego paused and raked a hand through his hair. 'On the day Eduardo died I'd had a furious argument with Alonso because he disapproved of my decision to become a professional polo player. I was in a foul temper,' he admitted grimly. 'It was a crazy idea to go out in my kayak when the river was swollen after the spring rains, and Eduardo tried to dissuade me. But I wouldn't listen, and eventually I shouted at him to leave me alone.'

Diego's throat felt raw, as if he had swallowed barbed wire, but now that he had started talking he could not stop the torrent. 'It was our first and only argument,' he said huskily. 'My last words to Eduardo were words of anger, and to my dying day I will never forget the expression of hurt on his face when I pushed him away.

'I continued up to the river alone, unaware that Eduardo had followed me. I didn't realise until I reached the bottom of the rapids, and turned and saw his empty boat carried along on the white-water.'

Lost in his private hell, he was unaware that Rachel had moved until he felt the light touch of her hand on his arm. 'Eduardo drowned?' she queried gently.

Diego nodded jerkily. 'The water was wild that day, and I imagine his boat must have overturned in the swirling current. We had both ridden the rapids many times before and knew what to do, but he must have hit his head on a rock. I got to the bank and raced back up the river…but I was too late.' His voice cracked. 'Eduardo was dead when I dragged him from the water.'

Oh, my love! Rachel wished she could say the words out loud, wished she could offer some sort of comfort to Diego, but the agony in his eyes told her that nothing could ease the devastation of losing his twin. Instead, she threaded her fingers through his and clung to him, and after a few moments he tightened his hand around hers.

'My mother was naturally distraught when I carried Eduardo's body back to the *hacienda*.' Diego spoke in a clipped tone as he fought to control the emotions surging through him. 'And my grandfather…' he closed his eyes briefly '…my grandfather accused me of deliberately causing Eduardo's death so that I could inherit the Estancia Elvira.'

'No!' Rachel could not restrain a cry at Alonso Ortega's cruelty. 'He must have known how much you loved your twin. And no one could have predicted that Eduardo would die in the river. It was a tragic accident.'

'An accident that I could have prevented,' Diego said harshly. 'Of course I did not mean for him to die, but if I had not been so headstrong, and Eduardo had not been so loyal, he would be alive today. He took his boat on the river to try and protect me—even though I had yelled at him.' His jaw clenched. 'You cannot know how that makes me feel,' he ground out, his voice throbbing. 'My grandfather was right. I killed my brother as surely as if I had stabbed him through the heart.'

'Diego, you can't believe that.' Rachel forced back the tears that were threatening to choke her. 'Everyone makes their own choices in life, and Eduardo *chose* to follow you down the river. It's a terrible thing that he died, but I don't believe he would have wanted you to spend your life racked with guilt.' Or to have become so emotionally damaged that he never allowed himself to become close to another human being, Rachel thought sadly. Diego had buried his heart with his twin, and it was little wonder he seemed so cold and aloof when his mother and grandfather had blamed him for Eduardo's death.

'That's why you don't live at the *estancia*, isn't it? There are too many memories of the past,' she said softly.

For the first time since he had bared his soul to Rachel, Diego forced himself to look at her, certain he would see disgust in her eyes for what he had done. But there was only understanding in her bright blue gaze, and a deep compassion that brought a lump to his throat. At least she did not hate him, as his mother and grandfather had done, and she seemed determined to absolve him of blame. But he blamed himself—and he always would.

'Sometimes, when the wind whistles through the trees, I swear I can hear the scream my mother gave when she saw Eduardo's body,' he said in a low tone. 'After Eduardo's funeral I couldn't bear to be here and I moved away, played polo in just about every corner of the earth. But every night my dreams brought me back to the *hacienda* and I saw his body, lying grey and lifeless.'

Diego gave a faint shrug. 'I had no contact with my mother and grandfather during all that time, but when Alonso died four years ago I discovered that he had made me his heir. Coming back here was…hard.' Words could not explain how hard it had been to return to his childhood home, he thought grimly. 'At first I resolved to sell the *estancia*—but I couldn't. Eduardo loved this place, it was his birthright, and to sell it would have felt like the ultimate betrayal.'

He glanced down at Rachel's upturned face and thought how beautiful she was. Tears shimmered in her eyes, and he realised with a jolt that her tears were for him.

'Do you understand now why I can't live here?' he asked jerkily. 'This should have been Eduardo's home.' And Eduardo should have had a beautiful wife and a child. His eyes were drawn to Rachel's swollen stomach. He knew she was finding these last few weeks of her pregnancy tiring, but she never complained, in the same way that she had not complained about moving to a new country and starting a new life. He had never told her how much he admired her for the way she had coped, he brooded. He had simply shut her out, as he shut everyone out. She deserved more than that, but he could not give her more. He was empty inside.

'Rachel…' While he had been wrapped up in his own thoughts she had turned very pale, and he saw a spasm of pain cross her face. 'I'm sorry,' he said gruffly. 'I know you hoped to stay here.'

She shook her head. 'It's all right. I think you are wrong to blame yourself for Eduardo's death, and I also think he would have wanted you to be here,' she said gently. 'But I understand why you would prefer to go back to the city, and I'm sorry I sent Arturo away.'

Rachel managed a faint smile, wanting to reassure Diego, but she felt another curious sensation in her lower stomach like the one she had felt a few moments ago, and she caught her breath as a sudden searing pain tore through her, so intense that she doubled over.

'What's wrong?' Diego demanded urgently. 'Are you in pain?'

'It's nothing,' she muttered, standing upright as the spasm passed. 'I think it must have been one of those practice contractions, in preparation for the real thing. The lady at the birthing class said you can have them for weeks before the birth. They're called Braxton Hicks contractions.'

'*Santa madre!* I don't give a damn what they're called,' Diego said explosively. 'I just don't want you having them here, miles from anywhere.' He dragged his hand through his hair. 'Wait here while I go and call Arturo. I've left my mobile at the stables and the only phone in the house is downstairs.' He strode across the room but paused in the doorway and turned back to her. 'Rachel…thank you.'

She understood immediately that he was thanking her for not denouncing him as a murderer as his mother and grandfather had done. Tears pricked her eyes but she gave him a wobbly smile. 'Go and make that call.'

She heard him thunder down the stairs and wanted to call

out that there was no need to panic, but just then another spasm ripped across her abdomen and she stifled a cry. She hadn't expected the practice contractions to be so strong and did not relish having them for the next few weeks. Her backache was agony and another spasm, worse than the two previous ones, almost made her legs buckle. She bit down on her lip so hard that she tasted blood, and tried to breathe calmly. But as the contraction finally passed she became aware of wetness between her legs and a bolt of fear shot through her as she realised with a sense of numb disbelief that her waters had broken.

Diego slammed down the phone and swore savagely before he ran back upstairs. 'Arturo will be a while. There's been a serious accident on the freeway and he says the traffic is…hell,' he finished slowly, his brain struggling to comprehend the sight of Rachel sitting on the bed, her head thrown back on the pillows and her legs drawn up.

'*Dios!* What are you doing?'

Sweat was pouring down her cheeks and her face was screwed up in an expression of agony, but it was the note of fear in her voice that made his gut clench as she gasped, 'Diego…I think I'm in labour.'

The paralysis that had temporarily gripped Diego's muscles eased. 'No, *querida*, it's just the practice contractions,' he reassured her. 'The baby's not due for another four weeks.'

'But it's coming now.' Pain ripped through Rachel's body and she could not hold back her cry. 'My waters have broken. The baby's coming, I know it is.' She stared up at him desperately, tears pouring down her face. 'I'm scared. It's too soon. And we can't get to the hospital.'

Diego quelled the fear coursing through him and knelt beside the bed, taking one of her hands in his. '*Querida*, even if you are in labour, first babies don't arrive that quickly. All the books say so. Arturo will come soon and we'll get you to the hospital, I promise.'

In reply Rachel let out a scream that tore at Diego's insides, and he watched in helpless disbelief as she tensed, her fingers clutching spasmodically around his hand. 'Our baby hasn't read the book,' she sobbed when she was able to speak. 'Diego, please…please, you've got to take my knickers off.'

The note of terror in her voice forced Diego to control his own fear. Rachel was in pain and he had to help her. Without another word, he jumped up, pushed her dress up to her waist and removed her underwear.

'*Santa madre,* I can see the head,' he said harshly. 'Rachel, I must get you to the hospital. The helicopter…'

'I'm not giving birth in a helicopter,' she gasped, her face screwing up once more as another contraction built to a crescendo of unbelievable pain. 'Oh, Diego, this is all my fault. I shouldn't have come, and I've put the baby in danger. There's no one here to help, but I can't give birth on my own,' she wept.

'You're not going to give birth on your own, *querida.*' Diego's voice was strong and calm, soothing Rachel's terror. 'I'm going to call the emergency services, but if they don't arrive in time I will deliver the baby.'

'Can you?' she asked waveringly, staring up at him with tear-drenched blue eyes.

There was no room for doubt, no time to remember that he had failed Eduardo. 'I can do anything,' he said steadily. 'Trust me, *mi corazon.*'

From then on Rachel lost all sense of time and the world became a blur of pain that sucked her under and threatened to overwhelm her. Her only anchor to reality was the sound of Diego's deep voice encouraging her and telling her that she was doing brilliantly, that she was the most amazing woman in the world.

'I want to push,' she groaned as the pain became deeper. 'Diego…I can't bear it…'

'Easy now, *querida,* easy now.' He spoke to her gently, as he would a frightened colt, trying to control the wild excitement flooding through him as he realised his child was about to be born. But something wasn't right. 'Rachel…' his voice was suddenly urgent '…the cord is around the baby's neck. You mustn't push yet. Do you understand me? You must wait.'

Racked with pain, Rachel put her arms above her head and gripped the rungs of the wrought iron headboard as she tried to recall the advice from her birthing class to pretend she was blowing out a candle. Short little breaths, short little breaths… 'I can't hold back,' she cried, panting as she desperately fought the primal urge to push.

'It's all right.' Diego snatched air into his lungs. 'Push now, Rachel.'

And, with a guttural scream, she did. Diego stared in utter wonder as the baby's head and shoulders emerged, followed by a tiny slippery body, and as he held his son in his hands his throat burned with the tears that slid unchecked down his face.

'We have a son,' he said in an awestruck voice. 'Rachel, we have a son.'

He looked up and saw the tears running down her cheeks. Wordlessly she held out her arms and, as he placed their child in her hands, their eyes met and held and he could not hide the emotions that were storming through him.

A thin cry broke the intense silence and as Rachel looked down at her tiny son she felt a tidal wave of love for him that swept away the doubts and fears she had harboured during her pregnancy. Nothing was more important than her baby, she thought mistily as she instinctively held him to her breast and felt a piercing joy when he suckled. He was worth every second of pain, and although he had been conceived by accident he was the most wanted, most adored baby in the world.

She looked up at Diego and her heart contracted when she saw that his face was wet. He was not emotionless, she thought sadly, but he had been so terribly hurt, and she did not know how to heal him. Her mind reran the birth, the frightening power of the contractions that she had felt were tearing her in two, and Diego's calmness and strength as he had held her. It could have gone terribly wrong, she thought shakily, remembering his sharp command not to push because the cord was round the baby's neck. Instinctively she hugged her newborn son to her and swallowed the lump in her throat.

'Our son owes you his life,' she said softly.

Pain flared in Diego's eyes. He could not tear his gaze from Rachel. Her hair was lank with sweat and she looked utterly exhausted, but her smile as she looked down at her son was the most beautiful thing he had ever witnessed. She was incredible, he thought deeply. And it had taken him far too long to appreciate how lucky he was to have her in his life—but he did not deserve her when Eduardo had nothing.

Rachel could sense Diego drawing away from her, retreating behind the barricades he had built around his heart, and she wanted to reach out to him and assure him that she would never hurt him as his mother and grandfather had done. But there was no time—and too much to say—and the sound of footsteps running up the stairs heralded the arrival of the paramedics.

'You had an amazingly quick labour for a first baby,' the paramedic commented when she had cut the cord and cleaned the baby, before wrapping him in a blanket. 'What are you going to call him?'

'I'm not sure,' Rachel murmured, stroking her finger over her son's petal soft cheek and his mass of downy black hair. 'I want him to have an Argentinian name.' Because Argentina would always be her child's home, she acknowledged. She had glimpsed the look of possessive pride on Diego's face as he had handed the baby to her, and she had known then that whatever happened between them, Diego would never part with his child. 'You choose,' she said shyly, giving Diego a tremulous smile. She wondered if he would want to name their son after his twin, but she did not like to suggest it.

After a second he said, 'Alejo is a good strong name—which complements his good strong lungs,' he added wryly, recalling his surprise that such a tiny baby had made such a loud protest when the nurse had washed him.

'Alejo Ortega,' Rachel tried it out and smiled down at the infant now sleeping in her arms. 'It's perfect.' He was perfect, and she would never ever leave him—which meant that she and Diego were stuck with each other, she thought sleepily, unable to fight the wave of exhaustion that swept over her.

'Are you happy?' she asked suddenly, staring at Diego and searching for some sign that would give her hope. But the wealth of emotion that had blazed in his eyes at the moment of Alejo's birth had disappeared, and the smile he gave her was cool and impersonal as he leaned over her and brushed his lips lightly over her cheek.

'Of course I am happy,' he murmured. 'You have given me a son. What more could I want?'

Me, Rachel wanted to cry. You could want me. But she said nothing and prayed he would think her tears were of happiness for her baby.

CHAPTER TWELVE

ALTHOUGH Alejo appeared in perfect health, despite his abrupt entry into the world, he was four weeks' premature and the paramedic was anxious to get him to the hospital in Buenos Aires as quickly as possible. Rachel did not argue. Her baby's well-being was paramount, but once she was in the ambulance she smiled down at her tiny son and whispered, 'You knew where you wanted to be born, didn't you, my angel. Now we just have to persuade your daddy that you should grow up on the Estancia Elvira.'

She spent a week in the exclusive private hospital Diego had booked, but felt a fraud when the nurses fussed around her because, apart from being a bit tired, she felt absolutely fine. Alejo had a mild case of jaundice—not unusual in premature babies, the doctor assured Rachel—but after phototherapy treatment, where he lay beneath an ultraviolet lamp, the baby quickly recovered and demanded feeding every two hours with a shrill cry that could not be ignored.

Back home, Rachel did her best, and Diego assisted in every way he could and frequently paced the nursery floor at two in the morning with his tiny son nestled into his shoulder. But, after a month of virtually no sleep, Rachel was hollow-eyed and painfully thin, and was inconsolable when the midwife suggested that she should supplement Alejo's feeds with baby formula.

'He was a low birth weight because he was early, but this baby is going to take after his father,' the midwife told her, glancing at Diego's six feet four frame. 'Alejo will do just fine on bottled milk; it's you I'm worried about,' she said, her beady eyes skimming over Rachel. 'You've lost too much weight.'

'I'm naturally thin,' Rachel defended herself. Privately she was amazed that her once huge stomach was now as flat as it had been before she'd fallen pregnant, and that she was already able to wear her jeans again. But she was exhausted and permanently anxious about Alejo, and her disappointment that she could not breastfeed him properly was made worse when Diego announced that he had hired a nanny.

'I don't need a nanny. I want to care for my baby myself,' she snapped, before bursting into tears.

'Post-baby blues are very common for new mothers in the first weeks after the birth,' the midwife had explained to Diego when he had managed to snatch a word with her out of Rachel's earshot. But he could not allow the situation to continue. Rachel was wasting away before his eyes and something had to be done.

'Ines will give Alejo his evening feed and be responsible for him during the nights,' he told Rachel implacably.

'Why can't I give his evening feed?' Rachel demanded sulkily, hating the idea of someone else looking after her baby, but at the same time acknowledging that most days she couldn't think straight because she was so tired.

'Because in the evenings you will do your hair and make-up and change into one of the new dresses I ordered for you, and we will go out for dinner.' Diego's eyes gleamed with determination at Rachel's mutinous expression. 'You're not just a mother, *querida*. You are also a wife, and you have a husband who wants to spend some time with you.'

Rachel was so stunned by this statement that, once she had met Ines, and discovered her to be both friendly and highly experienced in child care, she stopped fretting about leaving

Alejo for a few hours. It was good to wear normal clothes again, instead of maternity dresses. Diego had taken her for fittings at several of the top design houses and now her wardrobes were full of smart day-wear and exquisite evening gowns that showed off her slender figure.

The first evening they went out she was armed with a mobile phone and a spare in case Ines needed to contact her, but when she sat opposite Diego in one of the city's most exclusive restaurants it struck her that this was the first proper date they had ever been on. They had eaten out regularly when she had first arrived in Argentina, but then she had been preoccupied with her pregnancy. Now she no longer felt fat and ungainly, and in her sexy new clothes she felt like an attractive woman for the first time in months.

Had Diego even noticed? she wondered, peeping at him over the top of her menu. He glanced up from the wine list and she smiled at him and shook back her hair, excitement shooting through her when she saw his eyes linger on the low-cut neckline of her dress. Her breasts were a lot smaller than during her pregnancy, she thought ruefully. But the flare of heat in his eyes was unmistakable, and heat pooled between her thighs as she wondered if tonight he would ask her to share his bed for the first time since Alejo's birth.

They enjoyed a leisurely meal and, although their conversation revolved around their new son, Rachel felt closer to Diego than she had done for weeks. He seemed more relaxed tonight. Earlier in the day, when he had helped her bath Alejo, he had told her how he and Eduardo had delighted in flooding the bathroom at the *hacienda* when they had been young boys. Seizing the moment, she had encouraged him to recount more tales from his childhood and he had done so, laughing at the memories of the escapades he and Eduardo had got up to. Afterwards, when they had tucked their son into his crib, Diego had looked at her intently.

'I had forgotten all the good times I shared with my

brother,' he admitted. 'Or maybe I deliberately pushed them away because they were too painful to recall.'

'Are they painful now?' she'd asked softly.

He had sounded faintly surprised as he replied slowly, 'No—they're good memories, and I don't want to lose them.'

They lingered over coffee and in the soft glow of the candle flickering on their table Diego's eyes gleamed like polished gold. 'You look stunning tonight,' he murmured. 'You have regained your figure, and that dress shows off your tiny waist perfectly.'

'Thank you.' Rachel's heart was beating so hard she was sure it must be visible beneath her blue silk dress. She held her breath when he reached across the table and took her hand in his, idly rubbing his thumb over the pulse jerking in her wrist.

'I have a present for you—a little token of thanks for giving me my adorable son.'

At the sight of the small velvet box Rachel quickly schooled her features into one of appreciation, but when Diego opened the lid to reveal a band of diamonds and brilliant blue gems she gave a gasp of genuine delight. 'Oh, Diego, it's lovely.'

'The sapphires are from Sri Lanka and are a lighter blue than most other sapphires,' he explained. 'They are the colour of your eyes, *querida*.' He slid the ring onto her third finger, next to her wedding band. 'I noticed that you don't wear your engagement ring because it catches on Alejo's clothes. This is small and dainty, and I think it suits you better,' he said with a smile.

'I love it,' Rachel assured him. She loved him too, but she swallowed the words and picked up her coffee cup, unable to disguise the slight shake of her hand.

Diego glanced at his watch. 'It's getting late. I'll ask for the bill.'

'We don't have to leave yet. Maybe you would like a liqueur,' she said quickly, wishing that the evening would never end. 'I'm not the least bit tired.'

'I'm glad to hear it,' Diego said gravely, conscious of the strong, deep thud of his heart. 'I was wondering if I could interest you in a game of chess when we get home. Argentinian rules,' he murmured dulcetly, his eyes glinting wickedly as soft colour flooded her cheeks.

'I think you mean your rules,' Rachel choked, unable to hold back a smile as she remembered the chess games they had played during the heady days of their affair back in Gloucestershire. 'When I play chess with you I seem to lose my clothes.'

Diego walked around the table and drew her to her feet. 'That is the plan, *querida*,' he murmured, before he bent his head and brushed his mouth over hers in a kiss that left her aching for more.

They did not speak on the drive back to the apartment, but the silence shimmered with sexual tension that was almost tangible. Diego kissed her again when they stepped into the lift, and did not take his lips from hers until they reached the forty-second floor.

'I should check on Alejo,' Rachel whispered as he swept her up into his arms and carried her purposefully towards the master suite.

'Ines is in charge during the nights,' Diego said firmly. When he claimed her mouth once more Rachel could not resist him, and curled her arms around his neck as he strode into the bedroom and kicked the door shut behind them.

He might not love her as she loved him, but he cared for her, she was sure of it, she thought as he drew the straps of her dress over her shoulders and slowly revealed her breasts. He had given her an eternity ring, and Diego of all people would not have made such a gesture lightly.

'I thought we were going to play chess,' she teased as her dress slithered down her thighs and pooled at her feet.

'Revised rules,' he murmured against her throat. 'No playing board or pieces, and we both lose our clothes.'

He made love to her with exquisite care, conscious that it was only six weeks since she had given birth.

'You were so brave when you had Alejo,' he said deeply, shuddering at the memory of her lying on the bed, torn apart with pain. He would have given anything to have changed places with her and spared her the ordeal, and he had felt so helpless, but Rachel had coped brilliantly and had left him awed by her physical and mental strength.

'I wasn't brave, I screamed my head off,' Rachel said ruefully. 'I was so glad you were with me.' Her heart jolted when she met his gaze and saw an expression there that she could not define. But then he claimed her mouth once more in a drugging kiss, and she parted her lips and welcomed the bold sweep of his tongue, every nerve-ending in her body tingling with anticipation. He traced his hands over her breasts and her flat stomach, and then slipped between her thighs and stroked her gently through the sheer lace of her knickers.

'Diego…' It wasn't enough, not nearly enough. She was shaking with need, and she tugged frantically at his shirt buttons so that he laughed huskily at her eagerness and quickly stripped out of his clothes. He drew her panties down and then lifted her and laid her on the bed, desire pulsing through him as he nudged her legs apart. She was wet for him, but he was intent on arousing her fully and he bent his head and flicked his tongue over her taut nipple, heard her gasp of pleasure and transferred his mouth to her other breast. She had given him so much, he acknowledged as he gently parted her and slid his finger between her velvet folds, caressing her until she arched her hips. Rachel was like a golden light in his life, which had been dark for so long, and because of her gentleness and understanding he was slowly coming to terms with his past.

'Diego…now…please,' Rachel implored him as his wickedly inventive fingers made her quiver with longing to feel him deep inside her.

'I don't want to hurt you.'

'You won't…' She stretched her legs wide and sighed her pleasure when he eased into her, his hard length filling her while her heart flooded with love for him. After all that had happened to him, he might never be able to love her, but she understood now why he sometimes appeared distant, and she would always be there for him, no matter what.

He kissed her again, his mouth fused with hers while he drove into her in a steady rhythm that grew quicker and more intense with each deep stroke, until Rachel hovered on the edge of heaven, waiting for him to join her. She saw his head go back, the cords on his neck standing out as he gave one final thrust, and he cried her name as they fell together, their bodies trembling with the intensity of their passion. And, in the aftermath, Diego traced his lips over her cheek and hair and closed each of her eyelids with a gentle benediction, and she fell asleep in his arms, unaware that he lay watching her for long into the night.

For the next week Rachel was happier than she had ever been in her life. She spent her days caring for her darling son, but her nights were Diego's, and she certainly wasn't complaining about the dedication he showed to making love to her.

But her bubble burst when she woke one morning and saw him walking out of the en suite bathroom dressed in his riding gear.

'I'm sorry, sweetheart, but it's time for me to go back to work,' he murmured as he leant over the bed and dropped a soft kiss on her mouth. 'I'm due to play in a tournament in Brazil, and the sponsor's called to ask me to fly to Sao Paulo a couple of days early.'

His words came as an unwelcome reality check to Rachel. 'You intend to continue with your polo career, then?' she said slowly.

Diego looked surprised. 'Of course. Why wouldn't I?'

'It's a dangerous sport, and I thought…now that there is Alejo to consider, you might retire from competitions.'

He gave a faint shrug. 'Polo is no more dangerous than many other sports. Playing polo is what I do, Rachel,' he said a touch impatiently when she stared at him with an air of reproach that tugged at his insides. For the past ten years his career had been the one thing he'd been proud of, and if he was honest he had made polo his life. He hadn't thought about retiring, but he admitted to himself that he had left it this late to announce that he was flying to Brazil because he was reluctant to leave Rachel.

'Alejo will miss you,' Rachel said dully, trying to hide her disappointment that Diego would continue to spend much of his life travelling around the world to play in matches, and seemingly intended to leave her behind.

'I will miss him too…' Diego hesitated. 'When I come back, the Estancia Elvira is hosting a national tournament. I thought you would like to come with Alejo, and we'll spend a few days there.'

Rachel nodded and forced a smile, but during the following week while he was away she could not shake off the nameless dread that something would shatter her newfound happiness. Diego was an experienced player, she reminded herself. But he was also a dangerously confident rider who took risks other players would not dare.

Diego's flight from Brazil was delayed and he did not arrive at the *estancia* until the day of the national tournament. Arturo had driven Rachel to the *hacienda* two days earlier, the car laden with Alejo's stroller and crib and a mountain of other baby paraphernalia.

The housekeeper, Beatriz, adored the baby, and once Rachel had fed Alejo and settled him in his crib she went to find her husband. The stables were a hive of frantic activity and she searched desperately for Diego, her heart pounding when she caught sight of him striding across the yard, looking utterly gorgeous in pale jodhpurs and a black shirt and boots.

She loved him so much it scared her, she acknowledged as she forgot any pretence of acting cool and hurtled into his arms.

'Can I take it you missed me, *querida*?' he asked, his amber eyes glinting with amusement that swiftly turned to hunger as he claimed her mouth in a passionate kiss and she responded unrestrainedly.

'Of course I did,' she admitted shyly, unable to lie to him or hide her emotions any longer.

He set her down on her feet and stared at her, his expression suddenly so grave that her heart lurched painfully in her chest. 'Rachel…we need to talk,' he said in a strained voice. 'But not now,' he added with a grimace. The grooms were leading the polo ponies out and the babble of voices, horses neighing and the general air of pre-match excitement made conversation impossible. 'I have to go.' He dropped a brief, hard kiss on her lips and strode away to mount his horse, leaving Rachel staring after him, wondering what it was that he needed to say to her.

Had he realised that she was in love with him, and intended to warn her that he could never feel the same way? She already knew that, she reminded herself. But all the joy she'd felt at seeing him again had faded, and her heart felt like lead when she walked down to the polo field.

The national championships had attracted a huge crowd of spectators who filled the stands, while in the refreshment marquees the champagne was flowing. Rachel made her way to the opposing team's end of the pitch where, as top goal scorer, Diego was sure to be in action. The horses were snorting and pawing the ground and as soon as the umpire bowled the ball into play they began to thunder down the pitch.

It was exciting and terrifying to watch and, although Rachel had never played polo, she knew just how much skill was needed to halt a horse in full gallop, turn on a sixpence and hurtle off again, all the while trying to hit a small ball with a wooden mallet. Diego was an outstanding player who rode with a fearlessness which bordered on recklessness. He dominated the game and Rachel struggled to keep sight of him as he raced up and down the pitch so fast that his horse's hooves sent lumps of turf flying up into the air.

The accident happened so fast—and yet to Rachel, watching Diego's horse collide with another pony, he seemed to fly out of his saddle in slow motion, there was a tangle of legs and his horse hit the ground and rolled over, appearing to crush Diego beneath its massive body. For a few seconds a shocked silence gripped the crowd and then the air reverberated with cries and shouts, a woman screaming. Rachel did not realise at first that the screams were coming from her throat, she was simply calling Diego's name over and over as she fought to scramble over the barrier onto the pitch and was held back by a pair of strong arms.

'The paramedics are already with him,' one of the *gauchos*, Hector, said urgently. 'You can do nothing Señora Ortega. Go back to the *hacienda* and I will bring news as soon as I have a report of his injuries.'

'I can't leave him,' Rachel cried desperately. 'I want to be with him.'

But Hector shook his head grimly, and Rachel felt sick with fear. She knew the risks. Only a few months ago a top polo player from the US team had been killed during a match. She pressed her hand to her mouth to hold back her sobs. 'I have to go to him,' she choked.

'Go to your son, *señora*,' Hector told her harshly. 'I will come when I have news.'

Another of the ranch hands drove her back to the house. Rachel went without argument, knowing that Hector was right—there was nothing she could do for Diego, and she needed to be with her baby. The minute hand on the clock moved with excruciating slowness. Half an hour passed, an hour. Beatriz wept silently into her apron, but Rachel felt frozen inside as she fed and changed Alejo and forced herself to smile for him, while a voice in her head insisted—*he's not dead, he's not dead.*

The sound of tyres on the gravel drive made her heart stop beating and she rushed to the door, expecting to see Hector, her legs threatening to give way when Diego walked up the veranda steps, his shirt covered in dust and a livid purple bruise along one cheekbone, but otherwise apparently uninjured.

'Hello, *querida*.' Diego's gaze settled on her ashen face and red-rimmed eyes and he felt a pain in his chest that had nothing to do with his riding accident. When he had hit the ground and realised that he was about to be crushed by his horse, his one thought had been that he hadn't told Rachel what she meant to him—and in that split second he had known how desperately he wanted to live.

'I thought you were dead,' Rachel whispered, her throat feeling as though she had swallowed barbed wire. 'I watched the horse go down and I was sure you must have been crushed.'

'I saw it fall and knew I had to decide which way to roll,' he replied. 'Fortunately, I made the right choice. I'm fine,' he assured her gently when she stared at him as if she still believed he was a ghost. 'A couple of cracked ribs and a few bruises, including this beauty—' he ran his finger over his purple cheek '—but nothing to worry about.'

Nothing to worry about! The glib phrase hammered in Rachel's head as she recalled the worst hour of her life, when she had gone almost insane with worry, and her temper simmered.

She marched up to him, hiding her fury behind a sympathetic smile. 'Does the bruise on your cheek hurt?'

Diego gave a faint shrug. 'It's sore, but I'll live. Rachel…'

Her hand whipped through the air and cracked against his other cheek. 'Well, there's a matching bruise. Trust me, it doesn't hurt nearly as much as the pain I felt when I saw…when I thought…' Rachel's voice broke and tears streamed down her face as if a dam inside her had burst and released the flood of emotions she had tried to suppress during the agonising wait for news.

She stepped back, her eyes clashing with Diego's stunned gaze, and she felt sick when she saw the imprint of her fingers on his skin. But she was so angry—angrier than she had ever been in her life.

'How dare you put me through that?' she yelled at him. 'How dare you taunt death to come and claim you because you don't care if you live or die? I watched the way you rode today, with complete disregard for your safety. I know you still blame yourself for Eduardo's death. It was a tragic accident, Diego. It was not your fault. Yet you seem determined to be a martyr for the rest of your life.'

She paused to drag oxygen into her lungs, her whole body trembling, while Diego stood as still as if he had been carved from granite. 'Sometimes I wish I didn't love you,' she said brokenly. 'But I do, damn you. I do.'

She saw the sudden blaze in Diego's eyes and knew she had gone too far. He was probably furious with her. And, as usual, her tongue had run away with her. Blinded by tears, she spun round and hurtled up the stairs but, before she was halfway to the top, Diego caught up with her and she gasped when he snatched her into his arms. She could not bear to face him, not when she had revealed her feelings for him, and she beat her fists against his chest in fury.

'Go away. Leave me alone.'

'I can't do that, *querida*. I will never leave you again,' he vowed as he strode down the landing and kicked open the door to the master bedroom. 'You are my wife and we will never be apart again, not even for one night.' His voice throbbed with emotion, but as Rachel lifted her startled eyes to his face he brought his mouth down on hers and kissed her until she sagged against him and parted her lips so that his tongue could slide between them.

It was a kiss of possession and determined intent, his lips

moving on hers with bruising force as the storm between them raged out of control. Tears were still pouring down Rachel's cheeks as she relived her terror that she had lost him for ever, and she kissed him back hungrily, needing to taste him and know that he was really here and not some figment of her imagination. His hands roamed up and down her body, curving around her bottom to drag her against his pelvis, and then up over her hips and waist until he cupped her breasts in his palms.

Wild excitement coursed through Rachel when he tugged open the buttons running down the front of her sundress and bared her breasts to his burning gaze. The feel of his hands on her naked flesh felt so good, so right, and she wanted him so very badly. But nothing between them had changed, and the warning voice in her head battled with her feverish need for his possession.

'Diego…' He lifted his mouth from hers and she shivered when he trailed his lips over her jaw and down her throat. Her heart was breaking and if he took her to bed now she feared it would destroy her. 'I don't want to have sex with you.'

'I don't want to have sex with you, either, Rachel.'

'You…don't?' She thought she had suffered as much pain as she could bear, but his rejection was agony.

Diego cupped her face, his hands shaking, and stared intently into her eyes. And suddenly the words that he had wanted to tell her for so long were not difficult to say. 'I want to make love to you,' he said deeply. 'But first I need to tell you…that I love you, *querida. Te amo*, Rachel. *Tu eres mi vida, mi amor.*'

He brushed her tears away with his mouth and Rachel trembled when she saw the tenderness, the *love*, blazing in his eyes. 'If I'm honest, I think I fell in love with you when I scooped you up after you'd been thrown from your horse,' he told her softly, smiling faintly at the stunned disbelief in her eyes. 'You were tiny and beautiful, and so argumentative. I'd never met anyone like you before, and the month we spent together was the happiest of my life. But you proved just how different you were from my previous lovers when you walked out on me.

'It hurt,' he admitted gruffly. 'And I was so furious that you had the power to hurt me that I went to New York utterly determined to forget you. But I couldn't get you out of my mind, and when I heard that you had tried to contact me I seized on my business trip to London as an excuse to visit you.'

'And found me seven months pregnant with a child you refused to believe was yours,' Rachel murmured.

He winced. 'You did not deserve my anger, or my foul accusations, *querida*. At first I felt a fool for falling into the age-old trap, but when I calmed down I knew you had told the truth when you said you had been a virgin—and then I was angry with myself that I had not been more gentle that first time.

'Don't cry any more, *mi corazon*,' he said softly, grazing his lips over her damp cheeks. 'I never want to make you cry again. I felt that it was wrong to love you when I had robbed Eduardo of his future. And my guilt had been reinforced by my mother and grandfather, who accused me of being responsible for his death. I can never escape the fact that if I had curbed my temper that day, Eduardo would still be alive,' he said quietly. 'But you made me realise that my brother would not want me to waste my life in bitter recriminations and deny what is in my heart.'

More tears filled Rachel's eyes when she saw that Diego's lashes were wet. He would never fully recover from losing his twin, and his mother and grandfather had made his pain even greater. He had been alone for so long, but he would never be alone again.

'What is in your heart?' she whispered.

'You,' he said simply, his voice breaking with emotion as he enfolded her in his arms and held her so close that she could hear his heart beating unsteadily. 'You and Alejo are my reasons for living and I will love you both until I die.'

'Oh, Diego…' She stretched up on tiptoe, flung her arms

around his neck and pressed desperate kisses to his damp lashes, his bruised face, and hovered over the sensual curve of his lips. 'I love you so much it *hurts*.' She kissed his mouth and felt a piercing joy when he groaned and kissed her back with a tender passion that promised love and commitment that would last for eternity.

'Make love to me,' she pleaded, and he laughed joyfully, his mouth on her breast as he pushed her back onto the bed and covered her with his big body.

'With pleasure, *mi amante*.'

Their clothes were an unwelcome barrier he swiftly removed, and his amber eyes glittered with desire as he stared down at her pale, slender body and then nudged her thighs apart and moved over her. 'I love you, my Rachel,' he whispered against her mouth as he entered her. And he repeated the words over and over, making love to her with his heart, mind and body and with all the love inside him until they reached the heights together and drifted slowly down to lie blissfully content in each other's arms.

Diego idly wrapped a strand of Rachel's hair around his finger. 'I think we should make the Estancia Elvira our permanent home. It will be good for Alejo to grow up here,' he murmured, his heart turning over at the undisguised happiness on her face. She was so beautiful, and he loved her so much. He would never let any harm come to her or his son, he vowed fiercely.

'Are you sure you want to?' she said softly.

'I'm certain.' There were no ghosts here now, only happy memories of Eduardo. 'My competition days are coming to an end, and I want to be more involved with the day to day running of the ranch. Besides, once you've seen the present I've bought you, I doubt I'll ever be able to drag you away from the stables.'

Rachel smiled at him. His love was the only gift she wanted, but curiosity got the better of her. 'What present?'

'A showjumper—seventeen hands, black, apparently his name means "dark"…'

'Piran?' Rachel gasped. 'Really? Oh…Diego…' she buried her face in his neck, feeling as though she would explode with joy '…I love you.' Words were so inadequate to express what she felt, but he understood.

'I know, *querida*. And I love you too. Always and for ever.'

* * * * *

*Turn the page for an exclusive extract
from Harlequin Presents®*
THE SHEIKH'S FORBIDDEN VIRGIN
by
Kate Hewitt

Taken by the sheikh for pleasure—but as his bride…?

At her coming-of-age at twenty-one, Kalila is pledged
to marry the Calistan king. Scarred, sexy Sheikh Prince
Aarif is sent to escort her, his brother's betrothed, to
Calista. But when the willful virgin tries to escape, he
has to catch her, and the desert heat leads to scorching
desire—a desire that is forbidden!

Aarif claims Kalila's virginity—even though she can
never be his! Once she comes to walk up the aisle on
the day of her wedding, Kalila's heart is in her mouth:
who is waiting to become her husband at the altar?

A LIGHT, INQUIRING KNOCK SOUNDED on the door, and, turning from that grim reminder, Aarif left the bathroom and went to fulfill his brother's bidding, and express his greetings to his bride.

The official led him to the double doors of the Throne Room; inside, an expectant hush fell like a curtain being dropped into place, or perhaps pulled up.

"Your Eminence," the official said in French, the national language of Zaraq, his voice low and unctuous, "may I present His Royal Highness, King Zakari."

Aarif choked; the sound was lost amid a ripple of murmurings from the palace staff, who had assembled for this honored occasion. It would take King Bahir only one glance to realize it was not the king who graced his Throne Room today, but rather the king's brother, a lowly prince.

Aarif felt a flash of rage—directed at himself. A mistake had been made in the correspondence, he supposed. He'd delegated the task to an aide when he should have written himself and explained that he would be coming rather than his brother.

Now he would have to explain the mishap in front of company—all of Bahir's staff—and he feared the insult could be great.

"Your Eminence," he said, also speaking French, and moved into the long, narrow room with its frescoed ceilings and bare walls. He bowed, not out of obeisance but rather respect, and heard Bahir shift in his chair. "I fear my brother, His Royal Highness Zakari, was unable to attend to this glad errand, due to pressing royal business. I am honored to escort his bride, the princess Kalila, to Calista in his stead."

Bahir was silent, and, stifling a prickle of both alarm and irritation, Aarif rose. He was conscious of Bahir watching him, his skin smooth but his eyes shrewd, his mouth tightening with disappointment or displeasure, perhaps both.

Yet even before Bahir made a reply, even before the formalities had been dispensed with, Aarif found his gaze sliding, of its own accord, to the silent figure to Bahir's right.

It was his daughter, of course. Kalila. Aarif had a memory of a pretty, precocious child. He'd spoken a few words to her at the engagement party more than ten years ago now. Yet now the woman standing before him was lovely, although, he acknowledged wryly, he could see little of her.

Her head was bowed, her figure swathed in a kaftan, and yet, as if she felt the magnetic tug of his gaze, she lifted her head and her eyes met his.

It was all he could see of her, those eyes; they were almond-shaped, wide and dark, luxuriously fringed, a deep, clear golden brown. Every emotion could be seen in them, including the one that flickered there now as her gaze was drawn inexorably to his face, to his scar.

It was disgust Aarif thought he saw flare in their golden depths, and as their gazes held and clashed he felt a sharp, answering stab of disappointment and self-loathing in his own gut.

* * * * *

Be sure to look for
THE SHEIKH'S FORBIDDEN VIRGIN
by Kate Hewitt,
available October from Harlequin Presents®!

HARLEQUIN *Presents*

TWO CROWNS, TWO ISLANDS, ONE LEGACY

A royal family torn apart by pride and its lust for power, reunited by purity and passion

Look for the next passionate adventure in
The Royal House of Karedes:

THE SHEIKH'S FORBIDDEN VIRGIN
by Kate Hewitt, October 2009

THE GREEK BILLIONAIRE'S INNOCENT PRINCESS
by Chantelle Shaw, November 2009

THE FUTURE KING'S LOVE-CHILD
by Melanie Milburne, December 2009

RUTHLESS BOSS, ROYAL MISTRESS
by Natalie Anderson, January 2010

THE DESERT KING'S HOUSEKEEPER BRIDE
by Carol Marinelli, February 2010

HARLEQUIN *Presents*

EXTRA

DARK NIGHTS WITH A BILLIONAIRE

*Untamed, commanding—
and impossible to resist!*

Swarthy and scandalous, dark and dangerous, these
brooding billionaires are used to keeping women for as
many nights as they want, and then discarding them....

But when they meet someone who throws their best-laid
plans off track, will these imposing, irrepressible men
be brought to their knees by love?

**Catch all of the books in this fabulous
Presents Extra collection, available October 2009:**

The Venetian's Midnight Mistress #73
by CAROLE MORTIMER

Kept for Her Baby #74
by KATE WALKER

Proud Revenge, Passionate Wedlock #75
by JANETTE KENNY

Captive In the Millionaire's Castle #76
by LEE WILKINSON

HPE1009

When a wealthy man takes a wife,
it's not always for love…

Miranda Lee

presents the next installment in the
Three Rich Husbands trilogy

THE BILLIONAIRE'S BRIDE OF CONVENIENCE

Book #2860

Available October 2009

Find out why Russell, Hugh and James, three wealthy
Sydney businessmen, don't believe in marrying for love,
and how this is all about to change.…

Pick up the last passionate story
from this fabulous trilogy,

**THE BILLIONAIRE'S
BRIDE OF INNOCENCE**
November 2009

HP12860

**Stay up-to-date
on all your romance
reading news!**

The Harlequin
Inside Romance
newsletter is a **FREE**
quarterly newsletter
highlighting
our upcoming
series releases
and promotions!

Go to
eHarlequin.com/InsideRomance
or e-mail us at
InsideRomance@Harlequin.com
to sign up to receive
your **FREE** newsletter today!

REQUEST YOUR FREE BOOKS!

HARLEQUIN *Presents*®

2 FREE NOVELS PLUS 2 FREE GIFTS!

PASSION
GUARANTEED
SEDUCTION

YES! Please send me 2 FREE Harlequin Presents® novels and my 2 FREE gifts (gifts are worth about $10). After receiving them, if I don't wish to receive any more books, I can return the shipping statement marked "cancel". If I don't cancel, I will receive 6 brand-new novels every month and be billed just $4.05 per book in the U.S. or $4.74 per book in Canada. That's a savings of close to 15% off the cover price! It's quite a bargain! Shipping and handling is just 50¢ per book*. I understand that accepting the 2 free books and gifts places me under no obligation to buy anything. I can always return a shipment and cancel at any time. Even if I never buy another book, the two free books and gifts are mine to keep forever.   106 HDN EYRQ 306 HDN EYR2

Name	(PLEASE PRINT)	
Address		Apt. #
City	State/Prov.	Zip/Postal Code

Signature (if under 18, a parent or guardian must sign)

Mail to the **Harlequin Reader Service:**

IN U.S.A.: P.O. Box 1867, Buffalo, NY 14240-1867
IN CANADA: P.O. Box 609, Fort Erie, Ontario L2A 5X3

Not valid to current subscribers of Harlequin Presents books.

Are you a current subscriber of Harlequin Presents books and want to receive the larger-print edition? Call 1-800-873-8635 today!

* Terms and prices subject to change without notice. Prices do not include applicable taxes. Sales tax applicable in N.Y. Canadian residents will be charged applicable provincial taxes and GST. Offer not valid in Quebec. This offer is limited to one order per household. All orders subject to approval. Credit or debit balances in a customer's account(s) may be offset by any other outstanding balance owed by or to the customer. Please allow 4 to 6 weeks for delivery. Offer available while quantities last.

Your Privacy: Harlequin Books is committed to protecting your privacy. Our Privacy Policy is available online at www.eHarlequin.com or upon request from the Reader Service. From time to time we make our lists of customers available to reputable third parties who may have a product or service of interest to you. If you would prefer we not share your name and address, please check here. ☐

HP09R

I ♥

HARLEQUIN *Presents*

BROUGHT TO YOU BY FANS OF
HARLEQUIN PRESENTS.

We are its editors and authors
and biggest fans—and we'd
love to hear from YOU!

Subscribe today to our online blog at
www.iheartpresents.com